GW00730070

"This brought home the reality of how innocence was once present in their-own lives, the hypnotic tones from the ice-cream van that is, and how lucky they were to have their 'own' children living a happy existence within a loving-family unit. And, without the threat of any outside influence that could smash their kindred spirit apart, like a priceless Victorian Vase slipping from a child's grasp, they were no less in heaven than God was."

The Ballad of Frank JR

Written by

David Hines

***

All characters in this novel are completely fictional. Any resemblance to any locations or people in The Ballad of Frank, Jr is purely coincidence 2nd Edition

©The Ballad of Frank, Jr

2 January 2021

Chapter One
Exposition

Frank closed his eyes and took in his first deep breath of freedom in over two years. "Well son," he said to himself "this day, my friend, is the first day of the rest of your life."

He let out a sigh of relief then glanced up towards the breaking sunshine. For a moment, it gave him the impression of a new day dawning, but autumn's familiar chill soon reminded him of darker days gone by. He brushed himself down and put his best foot forward.

"Well ... come on feet," he muttered.

Frank took a footslog towards the direction of his mother's house, taking in as much as possible from the environment which now surrounded him; a familiar street which was once used as a playground by himself, and two of his best pals, Mark and Dave; another era vanished into thin air, no less.

With his memories firmly intact, he marched on towards the mouth of Pinewood Avenue, egger to wash away any remnants of prison life in his mother's bathtub. He took out an old handkerchief and brushed his nose.

"Yes," Frank smiled and cleared his throat "I can't wait to have a good old soak; something I've been waiting for, for a long time."

Number 6 had an overgrown front garden which mainly consisted of a few grubby conifers; wild couch grass which slowly penetrated the neighbours freshly cut green; weeds, nettles and a bag of old grass cuttings. A picture of neglect standing out amongst all the other 'well groomed' houses in the street.

Before Frank pushed open the gate, he looked up towards the bedroom window and noticed the curtains were fully drawn; unusual considering it was nearly lunchtime. Without a moment's hesitation, he dragged the small wooden gate across the uneven slabs and made his way down the overgrown pathway towards the house.

Frank tapped on the door, not to loud, not to quiet, just enough to create a distraction for his mother. Mary quickly ran down the hallway and reached out for the handle, blind to who, or what may have been lurking on the other side. She slowly turned the latch, letting day light shine through into the hallway. It was at that moment, just as she was about to say: 'no thanks,

I'm not interested' she felt a closeness only a mother could feel towards their off-spring; a closeness that somehow reached out and touched her very soul. However, it was the site of Frank's silhouette obstructing the sun's rays which made her knee's tremble and her voice wobble. She slammed her hands upon her cheeks and through her mouth wide open, replicating, for one moment, Edvard Munch's Scream.

"Oh my God, thank the Lord," hollered Mary.

Frank, being a little overwhelmed himself, through his arms around his mother and hugged her so tight, it nearly took her breath away.

"Mother, mother, I've missed you so much!"

Frank pulled away for a brief moment then peered down towards the floor desperately trying not to shed a tear. As he did, he noticed his mother was a tad on the large side; overweight, if you like. Mary was so overjoyed by the site of her only son stood on the doorstep, but it had slipped her mind about the fact Frank had no idea about the pregnancy.

"Oh my God!" Frank yelled, nearly informing the whole street he was back from his two year absence, "what's going on here?"

Mary sniggered. "Sorry Frank, I knew there was something I'd forgotten to tell you?"

She then placed both of her hands on her huge balloon shaped belly, and gently massaged herself using a circular motion.

"Well Frank, this is not the result of too much cottage pie, I can tell you."

"Ha ha very funny mother ... how did this happen?"

"You know something Frank, that lodger idea of yours wasn't such a 'bad' idea, after all."

Mary sneered, then subconsciously looked up towards the bedroom window in a dreamy like state. Frank's jaw slowly lowered like a drawbridge on one of North Wales finest.

"A half Spanish step dad ... whatever next?" Frank picked his jaw back off the floor then quickly waved his hand across his face, desperately trying to brush away an annoying fly which was buzzing around his nostrils.

"You better get used to it Frank, Pedro's here to stay."

"But you're so large, mother. I've never seen you like this before."

"No, I don't suppose you have, Frank, given you're my only son. By the way, my waters could break at any time so let's get off the door step and go inside."

Mary patted her belly then grinned at Frank. She then quickly turned and walked back into the house before the curtain twitchers decided to prey on them, once again.

"Come on, son. Let's get you out of the cold and into the nice warm living-room. You can sit in my favourite chair whilst I make you a nice cup of tea, then you can tell me *all* about it."

Frank tried his upmost to make sure his mother didn't go short of money prior to his spell in the nick. Mary never really had a spouse on whom to lean, either, which made things a little tricky. However, when Pedro came along, her domestic situation became a lot more enjoyable to cope with. In hindsight, it was the best thing Frank could have done for his mother; suggest a lodger that is.

"I think you have a few things to tell me, mother. I can't believe you're pregnant. This was the last thing I expected. But yes, a nice cup of tea does sound just the thing I need at the moment. By the way, where's the daddy, is he around?"

"Actually he's in Spain on business, but he's due back Friday morning … you'll probably have to move in to a bedsit come the end of the week, Frank."

"Well I never. I still can't believe it; you, pregnant, and at your age."

"Don't be so cheeky you! I'm not that old! I've a few years left in me yet! Now leave your bags in the hallway and go and sit down. I'll be in a minute with your drink … and Frank,"

"Yes, mother,"

"Switch the TV on will you!"

Frank made his way into the living room towards the chair in question; a miscellaneous piece of furniture that Mary must have brought for the reclining motion. He sat down and made himself comfortable. Its only then he started thinking; wondering why on earth his mother wanted him out of the house before Pedro came back.

"I take it the spare bedroom has been converted into a nursery, mother?" Frank shouted through into the kitchen.

"I'm afraid so, Frank," replied Mary, as she popped her head back through into the living room "but if it wasn't for that, well, you would be welcome to stay for as long as you wanted. I wouldn't just turf you out for no reason.

Although, I wouldn't want the pair of you getting under each other's feet so early on in the relationship, either."

"True." said Frank, in a somewhat solemn response to his mother's *excuses*.

"It may even be a blessing in disguise, Frank, the fact you have to move out that is. Besides, I'm sure you'll want your own space at the moment to gather your thoughts."

"Again mother, you make sense."

Mary brought in Frank's tea and placed it on a small wooden table.

"Thanks mom," he said. "I must say, you certainly know what your son craves; a nice mug of tea only a mother can make, now that sounds like heaven. A hot soak wouldn't go a miss either. I haven't had a bath in two years, only showers in the nick you see."

"Yes well, that's all behind you now my dear, but don't worry about things at the moment. You can sleep here on the sofa for a few days while Pedro's away in Spain, but when he comes back …"

Frank suddenly pouted like spoilt child who had just been refused a lucky bag.

"Listen Frank, he's been here a couple years now, so I wouldn't like to just turf him out just because your prison sentence has expired. Don't worry. I have a little place lined up for you."

"A little place …" Frank facetiously slurred.

"…all you have to do is go to the housing office up the road and they will give you the details. Just ask for Tom. I told him you may pay them a visit on the day of your release. But you'll have to act quick, Frank, he won't keep it forever."

Frank took a sip of his tea then breathed out a sigh of relief. "Thanks, what would I do without you?"

He then turned towards his mother and smiled.

"Come on," he said, in an inquisitive manner, "how did you swing that?"

"Well, I have a friend who has a friend who knows a friend ...listen Frank!" she snapped, "just make sure you see it through, there's not much time as it is. Here's the deposit. I managed to save it from all the money you sent me. All in all there is five hundred pounds. That should cover the deposit and two weeks rent up front, which he'll probably ask for, if I know Tom … ahem!"

During Frank's stay in prison, he always made sure he sent his mother every penny he earned. However, what he didn't expect was for her to save it all ready for his release. Frank also spent a lot of time in prison thinking. He often wondered what path he would eventually find himself drifting down, taking into account the crime he had committed.

Mary squatted down next to Frank and slowly lifted his hand off the arm of the chair. She then grasped it tight and rested it next to her soft, tender cheek. She prepared herself for the delicate question which had been bothering her for some time. Mary glanced up at the photo of a young Sarah which she always kept on the TV unit, next to the video recorder. She turned to her son; he was also engrossed in the image of Sarah. She squeezed his hand a little to grab his attention.

"It's nice to see you again Frank after all this time. How are you? How have you been coping over the past two years? Do you still think about Sarah?"

Frank sat back in his mother's 'special' arm chair, and drifted off into a daydream.

The brightest star lit up the heavens like a hundred flood lights shining down onto a small recreational piece of park land. The lack of a cool breeze, however, really made the day feel like the height of summer. The neighbours were outside dressed in t-shirts and shorts mowing their front lawns; blasting the fresh fragrance of grass cuttings into the warm atmosphere creating the very nucleus of an unforgettable memory, for Sarah and her father.

Sarah wore her favourite vest that morning, which Frank brought in anticipation of the fine weather which was coming their way. The Pixy Pals, a new children's program was very popular with kids from the age of three and upwards. Sarah's favourite character, Mommy-Pixy, was printed on the front of her vest who she simply cherished and adored, just like any innocent seven year old child would.

Frank pulled up outside Dave's house and tooted his horn. He wondered if the sudden noise pollution from his little Mini Cooper could grab his attention just enough to entice him out of the house. Sarah on the other hand was too preoccupied in the back seat. The only thing she was interested in was trying to release her seat belt from its bear hug like grip.

"I hate these things, daddy," moaned Sarah.

"I can never get them off again once they're on. Daddy, help me will you!"

"Just press the red button down, Sarah!" Snapped Frank.

"I am, I am; it isn't working!"

***

"I'm okay to be honest," Frank turned back to face his Mother "you know what I'm like anyway; like a bouncy ball I am; throw me against the wall and see what happens."

"Son, you'll be fine. It was an accident. Ok, you had a few drinks, but you were very unfortunate, Frank."

"Yeah...."

"Don't think about it now, you're a free man and don't let anyone get to you either. You've paid you debt to society so you should be allowed to get on with your own life, in peace!"

"I know, I know, but I do feel a little guilty sometimes, especially now I'm a free man. Poor old Sarah ... and at the innocent age of seven. It should be me in the cemetery mother, not her! *"*

"Frank!"

"No, it's true! It should be me in there, not her! And the flashbacks I may have, according to the prison psychiatric nurse, may strike at any time!"

"What?"

"Flashbacks!"

"Of the car crash?"

"Yes!"

Frank slowly drifted into a monolog of melancholy, mumbling his way through what was slowly starting to sound like a confession to Mary.

"You see," Frank went on to say "the way I remember it is; I was driving down the dual carriageway talking to Sarah, who was looking at my reflection in the rear mirror; laughing, when suddenly the traffic lights quickly changed from amber, to red. It all happened in a split second and after that, well, it's all a blank to be honest."

Frank reminisced a little more.

"I just remember waking up in what seemed to be an ambulance. I thought this because I distinctively remember a blue flashing light illuminating the concerned bystanders. They just stood there mother, some panic stricken, some in tears."

Frank paused for a second...

"... they were all looking in the direction of a small torso which was laid out in the middle of the road. It was covered over with a small white blanket so I couldn't quite tell what was transpiring at that moment in time.

"Oh dear, Frank."

"I was well and truly drugged up with pain killers too, so wasn't in any position to ask questions. Of course, later on,
I realised that bump in the road ..."

Frank burst out crying.
"Come here son," Mary carefully
took Frank, and held him close to her bosom. "I will book an appointment at the doctors," she said, "maybe he will be able to help you?"

"No mother, it's ok ..."

Frank sat up straight and quickly composed himself.

"...you see, whilst I was having my therapy in prison, the therapist told me I may never remember the crash itself, so I may never understand what actually happened. It's like my mind has totally blocked it out. On the other hand, I could have a flash back at any time. It's that unpredictable she reckons."

Mary stared at Frank, concerned and slightly tearful at the things she had just heard. It was all a bit overwhelming for her because deep down she didn't really understand what her son was talking about, or how he really felt.

"I'll make the phone call, Frank."

"Honestly, I'll be fine. It's nice to know somebody cares though."

"Of course I care you nitwit."

Franks smiled at his mother then reached for his tea.

"Listen, Frank, you have a bedsit to see this afternoon, so let's get you in the right frame of mind. I'll go and run you a hot bath. Just finish off your tea ... and Frank,"

"Yes mother."

"Welcome home, my dear."

"Thank you mother, that's music to my ears."

Mary walked back towards the kitchen.

"Oh, by the way," Frank added, "why was your bedroom curtains shut when I arrived today?"

"Oh I don't know, Frank ... force of habit I suppose."

With his tea clutched in both hands for comfort and warmth, Frank sat back and relaxed in his mother's 'special' chair. He then took a

moment to mull over his mother's last comment
regarding *force of habit.*

"One more thing, Frank,"

"What's that then, mother?"

"Give me the TV remote. I'll find you a
decent channel to watch. I'm not being funny,
but there're loads of new programmes on. This
one you will like. It's a new chat show, but with
a difference.

"What do you mean?"

"Just watch and enjoy."

"You're the boss." replied Frank.

Mary switched to channel three making it
just in time to introduce her son to a brand new
American chat show. It was hosted by a young
mouthy guy going by the name of Jonny Jill.
Some folk thought he was a bully, the chat show
host that was, but Frank's mother loved him,
especially when he shouted back at the alcoholic
couples who had their young off spring in tow.
They would sit on the stage, or stand, according
to what mood they were in, and fight for their
right to live a normal life, all in front of a manic,
but unusually well-dressed audience. Frank put
his feet up and smiled to himself. He didn't want
to dispel the myth that prisons weren't equipped
with TV's, so just kept quiet. He leaned over and

grabbed the local free press that sat on a nest of wooden tables next to the chair. He had a half-hearted glance, but kept getting side-tracked by what was showing on TV: an audience of unemployed people debating clinical depression in front of four TV cameras and a worrying six million viewers, which now, unfortunately, included himself.

" … Force of habit," Frank whispered under his breath.

Chapter Two

The Housing Office

The queue itself was long and depressing as you might imagine in a council housing office. The waiting room was dull in lighting and the décor was either retro in style, or had basically never been touched in the last fifteen years; the latter seemed more realistic to Frank.

Frank managed to spot a place to sit. It was in the middle of a long padded wooden bench which stretched the length of the back wall. There was a large lady who had about four bags of food shopping, one of them full of what looked like wallpaper and paint brushes, sitting in the middle of the bench which took up most of the room. Frank managed to squash himself in between the said lady and a younger man, who was also quite large in size. The teenager in question, who didn't quite look old enough to be on the housing waiting list in the first place, wore music headphones and pretended not to acknowledge anyone around him, typical. However, Frank knew for a fact that as soon as his ticket number was called out, he would suddenly have the world's most sensitive hearing.

Whilst Frank tried his best to get comfortable on the bench, he suddenly noticed he was being eyeballed by an unseemly character. He had long dirty hair, which looked to Frank like it hadn't been washed in years. It was also quite flat on the one side of his head making the vagrant look quite hilarious at first glance. This was probably due to the fact he had been lying down on a park bench, or in a shop door way with nothing but a pile of newspapers for a pillow. He had a long khaki rain coat which stank to high heaven; he also wore brown pin-stripe trousers and boots, which were obviously a couple of sizes too large for him. It begged the question to where he got them from in the first place. More concerning to Frank though was the fact that he fashioned a gold wedding band on his finger, which seemed to fit perfectly.

Without so much as a blink of an eye, the character sat there, and stared directly at Frank. He tried his hardest to ignore him, but it was no good; the character was, how you say, determined. Frank quickly turned his head towards a public information poster to try and take his mind off the rude man. Unfortunately, it read: 'Think, before you drink, before you drive'. Not a good move, in hindsight.

"Great," Frank said to himself, "Just what I need to cheer me up."

Once again he turned to the stranger, fortunately for Frank he was fast asleep; it was either that or unconscious from drinking too much cheap cider, judging by the empty bottle he had in his grasp. This was a weight off Frank's mind. He could finally relax and chill-out for a while until his ticket number was called out.

He leaned back on the wooden bench and started to reminisce. He recalled the day he and Sarah arrived at Dave's party, one sunny afternoon, just over two years ago.

***

Frank turned around and pushed the button for Sarah, finally bringing the drama to an end thus releasing the seat belt. As he did, she quickly scrambled over the front passenger seat, out onto the grass verge, nearly treading in dog poo, then out on to the pavement where she was greeted by Dave.

"Ah, my special little friend," he whispered under his breath.

Sarah laughed, then nicely, but softly, pushed him away.

"Hi Dave, how are you?" she smiled then stuck her tongue out at him.

"Quickly," Said Dave, "run into the house; there's a few of your friends in the kitchen. The doors already open so don't worry…"

But before he had time to finish his sentence, Sarah was already halfway through the front doorway shouting "Hello, hello, is anybody there?"

"Hi Sarah," replied Mark.

Mark was the second person to see Sarah as she flew into the lounge nearly knocking Dave's new yucca plant over.

"Where's your daddy?" Mark snapped. "Oh, I can see him, he's walking up the pathway trying to grab Dave's can of beer out of his hand. Bloody hell, can't he wait until he gets into the house? They're two crates here waiting
to be demolished."

***

Frank obviously had to grin and bear all the reality checks, which hung over him like the Sword of Damocles, and patiently wait his turn.

After about five minutes he was finally called upon by a nice little lady named Alison. She was the one and only receptionist in the housing office. This made things a little difficult sometimes, especially if there was an unusually large queue of 'property seekers' to attend too.

Tom, on the other hand, was the assistant manager of North Birmingham District Housing Association. His main role was to make the big decisions like accepting housing applications, and of course, refusing them. Somehow though, Mary had 'swung it' so he could jump the queue and grab himself a roof over his head in record time … luckily for him.

"Afternoon, Mr. Langley I presume?"

"Hi, yes my name is Frank. My mother …"

"Take a seat, Mr. Langley. I will be with you in a minute."

Frank slowly weaved his way over to Tom's desk, which was safely located behind reception, and sat down.

After a brief two minute absence in the key cupboard, Tom arrived back at the desk then sat down opposite Frank.

"Here are two forms for you to sign, Mr. Langley. One is a six month contract for number 13 Edgewood Avenue, and the other is a declaration. That's basically saying you understand the contract and you except the terms and conditions."

The fat oversized housing manager, still out of breath from his short trip to the utility room, sat back in his chair and crossed his arms.

Frank quickly signed both copies, not giving a second thought to the rules and regulations he had just accepted. He then pushed the paper-work back across the desk towards Tom and smiled.

"The address is on your copy of the lease, it's also written on the plastic key fob. Any questions?"

"No!"

Frank stood up and offered Tom the formality of a handshake, but Tom just glared back at him; nodding his head in a 'what's the world coming too' type fashion. He then breathed out another deep-sigh of contempt towards Frank, and shook his hand.

That was the end of that. Short, sweet, and to the point. The job was done and Frank was no longer homeless.

Chapter Three

Dave and Mark on the job

During Frank's absence, Mark and Dave had grown quite close. Mark was well established within Dave's landscaping business, and Dave, well, he was happy enough. He had Mark on board, and for twenty pounds a day, he was laughing all the way to the bank.

Mark had left his safe, menial job as a book-binder two years previous. His father wasn't impressed when he first heard the news, but it was all a little too late to talk him out of it because he had already signed a contract with Dave.

Henry, Mark's dad, was the sort of bloke who liked to keep things under control, which, when you think about it, is quite normal for an anxious parent. When Henry found out there was no going back though, and his only son was well established within Dave's grasp, he went ballistic. He shouted at Mark and threatened to kick him out onto the streets, something, which fortunately for Mark, never reached fruition.

Dave ran his business for about four years. He started it back in 1990 after he was kicked out of house and home. The very process of flying the nest, albeit involuntary, suddenly sparked him into creating a small business to help pay the bills. The only skills he had were gained from his YTS days, so had no alternative but to dabble in a spot of Landscaping. His battered old pickup truck that he used to drive around from job-to-job, was his pride and joy. The only thing was the passenger seat was missing so whenever Mark went along with Dave, which was more often than not, he had to jump in the back and ride shotgun with Mr. shovel and co.

Mrs. Smith owned a huge house on the Birmingham Road. It was a five bedroom property with a double garage and a in-and-out stone gravel driveway. The back garden was huge; fifty metres in length and fifteen metres in width. The borders and rockery were laced with a range of assorted shrubs and conifers; looking colourful and pretty amongst their evergreen counterparts. It was just the fence. It was missing a few panels on the right hand side: enter Dave and Mark.

They turned up at Mrs. Smith's about midday to start the job. It was Mark who knocked on the door. He gave it his usual rat-ta-tat-tat and then stepped back one pace to join Dave.

Dave spun the lady a yarn, "Hello Mrs. Smith, how are you? I hope we're not too late."

"Well ... "

Dave butted in.

"We've had one heck of a morning," Dave gave Mark the wink, "what with one thing and another, but we're fine now."

"That's ok, come in," the lady said, "it's through the back on your right hand side, you can't miss it," Mrs. Smith chuckled, "there's a big gap where there's supposed to be three or four fence panels."

"Right you are, Mrs. Smith."

To be honest, Dave was a conman. He knew all the tricks in the book. First, he would stand in front of the fence and hold his chin in a sort of: 'this doesn't look good' type manner. He would then walk along the fence-line and push the posts at random to see if any of them were loose. Most of the time they were okay, but Dave would give a little tug to weaken them so they would rock back and forth. This would then allow them to approach the customer and suggest a few God-Fathers to hold the fence posts steady.

The God-Fathers (concrete posts) cost twenty pounds from the builders-yard. There was then a matter of labour cost. Dave used to charge thirty-pound in labour for each God-Farther, so it worked out to fifty-pounds all in all. On a good day Dave and Mark could fit about seven God Fathers to a rickety stretch of panelling, which would mean a profit of two hundred and ten pounds for the business.

"Come on!" ordered Dave, "let's get the tools off the truck. This is a straight forward job and the panels are already here! We could finish this for five if we play our cards right!"

"OK mate don't panic!"

Mark quickly ran back to the van to collect the tools: a hammer, nails, spirit level, spade, rammer, a plumb line and a couple of other things he thought they may need.

Mark always wore the same clothes in the work place, as did Dave, but Mark's clothes wasn't really suited for the environment. For a start, he wore a pork pie hat, which on its own looked ridiculous, and a tracksuit top; he always wore striped tracksuit top for work, that and skin-tight jeans. Somehow, Mark always managed to get himself into a right state; boy, the sweat used to pour out of him. Most of the time he stank of stale alcohol. Dave's clothes, on the other hand, were very suitable for the work they did: a pair of steel toe capped boots to protect his feet and a pair of tough combat trousers; very sensible, and very safe.

"That's it mate. You know the drill, if you'll excuse the pun. Start digging them holes and I'll mix up the muck!"

Dave started to mix the cement for the fence-posts, while Mark dug the holes and generally cleared the way for the new panels.

"I can't wait until we meet up with Frank and have a piss up, can you?" said Mark.

"I know mate, it's going to be a right crack. I swear Frank hasn't had a drink in two years. I wonder if he'll drink at the party?"

"I'm sure he will indulge in the odd can or two."

Dave laughed. "Ha ha, he will be gagging for it mate ... and the booze."

"Gagging for it!" Mark screamed.

"shh, Mark, the customer."

"Sorry mate."

" ... well, Frank is definitely out because he wrote to me with the date of his release," Dave went on to say, "he also said to wait for a phone call from him. He did say, however, he wanted the party to be on a Friday night, for some reason?"

"Has he phoned you yet?"

"No, not yet, but give him time. He's only been released today; he'll probably phone me later. I'll let you know as soon as he does though, don't worry."

"OK mate, let us know and I can prepare for the party. There's a few crates to be purchased, me thinks."

"Your right there Mark, a few crates indeed.

Mark whistled away to one of his favourite tunes, American Pie, whilst he wacked the ground with his rammer. Dave on the other hand, was more concerned about finishing the job and getting back home. He couldn't wait to watch a pre-recorded episode of Gladiators; he was obsessed.

"That's it Mark dig ... dig," Dave whispered under his breath. *"Jet is waiting for me."*

Chapter Four

Frank's trip to the High street

Frank took in a deep breath and debated whether to jump back into his car and make his way back his mothers, or carry on towards Smeggington. In other words, a short drive back to watch repeats of Jonny Jill, or a long awaited stroll around the High-Street to wallow in some past memories.

As he started his 'heavy on the legs' plod up towards Smeggington, he heard a deep rumbling sound coming from behind him; too loud to be a car, but definitely driven by diesel. As Frank turned his head, he was overcome by a huge dark shadow, like a moody cloud drifting by on an unpredictable summers afternoon. He took a quick peek over his shoulder. There, in front of him, was the number 12 bus which should he decide to ride, would get him to the High-Street in speedy time. Frank ignored the massive puffs of black-smoke coming from the exhaust of the bus and soldiered on. The driver was obviously in some sort of difficulty; crunching and grinding the gears like a novice panicking on his first driving lesson.

As Frank approached Six Ways-Island, Smeggington's main road junction, he turned right onto the High-Street and began his walk towards a dense crowd of shoppers. Around that time of day it mainly consisted of young teenage-mothers with pushchairs; business people and the odd drunk, or two.

He hiked through the slippery mob, like an experienced mountain climber negotiating the north face of Snowdon, as he did he saw a shop. It looked fairly modern, and the name above it read 'New-Street-Vinyl'.

As Frank walked in, he noticed the shopkeeper was stood behind a counter which was covered in 'old skool' graffiti art. His dress sense reminded him of the early eighties Hip-Hop era: a Fila tracksuit top which he left unzipped and an old retro baseball cap, worn backwards, of course.

Frank nodded his head towards the guy, who had his head buried what looked like a newspaper, and said 'Alright mate'. The guy nodded back at Frank, put his pasty down on the counter and quickly directed his attention back to his magazine, Hip Hop Monthly.

He scanned his eyes around the shop once again, taking in all the stock which was on display around the store. To be honest, Frank wasn't into Hip-Hop come the year 1994; he was more of a 'Brit-Pop' type guy, as was most people during that era.

These highly infectious Hip-Hop tunes, (the Electro's), however, was introduced to him by an old Pakistani school friend who regularly brought music tapes in to class for people to borrow. The whole Hip-Hop scene was a big part of Frank's life during his school days. But now, it was the Stone Roses just like the guy behind the counter, according to the huge letters splashed over the front of his t-shirt: 'I Am the Resurrection'; a fitting statement for a guy who had opened a small, but interesting little business specializing in early eighties Hip-Hop

"How's it going, mate?" said Frank.

"It's a bit slow at the moment, but that's to be expected considering the current climate ... oh, and the lack of appreciation for classic Hip-Hop!"

"I see you're into the early eighties stuff. You don't have any Electros in stock, do you?"

"No chance mate! If I did, they'd be over there with all the other rare records."

Frank peered over towards a rather large wooden cabinet which had two glass sliding doors at the front. Inside there seemed to be an assortment of albums: Grand Master Flash, The Sugar Hill Gang and what seemed like promo 12-inch records.

"To be honest," the guy went on to say, "I have the whole collection in my loft at home. They're worth a lot, as well."

Frank snapped out of his daydream and refocused his attention towards Break Beat Bobby', which, according to a feeble ID badge on the left side of his tracksuit top, was his street name.

"Wow, I used to love all that," Frank added "although, I do think Electro 1, 2, 3 and Crucial were my favourites."

"You won't get them anywhere mate! They're rare as fuck … and number 5 mate; number 5 was the best!"

Frank doubled his pace, dodging the push-chairs and blanking the Big-Issue sellers and made his way towards a crowed of intrigued shoppers.

As he got near, he realised that there was four of five men singing. "They must be buskers." he whispered to himself.

Frank managed to nudge his way in just enough to see what all the fuss was about. He could see it was a type of Barber Shop Quartet who seemed to be covering modern chart songs.

He looked up. There wasn't a cloud in sight; blue-skies as far as the eye could see. And what's more, the cool autumn sway, which brushed through the popular trees that lined the footpath of the high street, was like mother natures music box: Swirling golden brown foliage ... *those mini-whirl-winds of autumn.*

It was at that very point,
'Barber Shop Rock' as they were apparently called, kicked off with another song. They turned the volume up on their amplifiers and counted in to a surprisingly unusual version of 'Waterfall'.

As Frank enjoyed the unconventional Barber Shop style version of: *"she'll carry on through it all ... she's a waterfall,"* he glanced around at the mesmerised punters. As he did, to his surprise, he spotted an old school pal, Katey Madison. He stared for a while but couldn't pluck up the courage to

make his move. Frank looked back at 'Barber-Shop-Rock' thinking how bizarre it was, but couldn't concentrate on them fully because he knew that Katey was just meters
away. He needed a good conversational gambit to break the ice, something that was humorous but not shocking. Again, Frank looked
over towards Katey, but to his disbelief, she was gone.

"Oh no!" Frank cried out.

But before he had chance to digest his panic in to a mild-shower of melancholy,
he suddenly felt a firm slap on his back. He turned around quickly, nearly bursting out with a mouth-full of abuse to the person behind him. Luckily he didn't, because he suddenly found himself in the position of no return, that is, he was face to face with his long lost 'girlfriend'.

He screamed out: "Oh my God!"

Katey smiled then wrapped herself
around Franks torso like an octopus who had just caught its prey. Within seconds they were both embraced like two lovers still in locked in their honeymoon period; pecking each other on the cheek and periodically pausing for breath.

"Katey, you haven't changed one bit. You're still as pretty as a picture."

"Why thank you, Frank. You're not looking too bad yourself. The years have obviously been good to you."

"Yeah … well. Anyway Katey, what you up too? Let's look at you."

Frank took two paces back, nearly bumping into an old lady and her bag of vegetables, and scanned Katey up and down.

"You look … well, you look great. It just seems like yesterday when I used to walk you home from school … remember Katey?"

"Ha Ha, yes, I remember Frank. I still owe you a kiss if my memory serves me correctly."

"Katey, there is nothing wrong with your memory, believe me!"

Frank smiled at Katey then turned his head in the direction of the singers.

"These guys are something else. What do you reckon, Katey?"

"Yeah Frank, they certainly are. To be honest, I've been here for about twenty minutes listening to them. In fact, I was just about to trap when suddenly I noticed you standing there on your lonesome"

"I noticed you as well, but I was trying to think of something to say. I was never good at the old ice-breaker, but I see you haven't lost your touch."

"No, well ... you know me Frank. Never one to hang about thinking about it."

"Yeah, well, I do remember you stalling once when I asked you a said question."

"Frank let's get out of here, maybe go for a drink or something. It's a bit noisy and I can't quite hear what you are saying."

Frank grinned at Katey; a grin so cheesy, it would've put any seventies sit-com to shame.

"Ok, that sounds great," Frank winked at Katey then checked his watch. "Oh shit, listen. I've got to go and see my new bed-sit now!"

"What!"

"It's a long story, Katey, but I'll fill you in another time. Listen, will you meet me, I don't know, let's say Saturday in the café over the road there ... about midday? That should give me chance to get my act together. I may even put a splash of Insignia on, just for you."

"Ha Ha, you haven't lost your sense of humour then I see. Ok mate, listen, I'll meet you in the café at twelve Saturday. Don't be late Frank ... I hate waiting around for people."

"I can't wait! Catching up on old times is going to be fresh!"

"Cool. And Frank"

"What's that?"

"Cool is the word you should be using these days, not fresh. It's not 1985 you know."

"Sorry my dear, I'm sure."

" … anyway, we can go to the pictures after if you like," adds Katey, "There's a good film on called 'Pulp Fiction'. Can't think where I seen it advertised now, but I'm sure it will be worth a watch."

"Yeah, I've seen that advertised somewhere as well. It's a date then, if you'll excuse the pun."

"Pun excused. See you Saturday, Frankie boy."

Katey was about 5/5 in height, a little smaller than Frank and wore long-white summer cotton dresses; almost see-through if the sunlight were to catch them at the right angle. She had beautiful legs and a lovely figure to match; not too thin, and not too bulky. She often wore a deep-red lipstick too which made her stand out from the crowd; a real eighties lookalike. Some used to say she resembled a young 'Jackie Graham', only Katey's head always fashioned a spiral perm. It was never long and straight like our Birmingham bred eighties pop-star always insisted on. She also smelt great, well; different. I mean, her cent was of a mature fragrance which wasn't something you could find in the teenage section of the chemist. Frank was convinced she wore her mother's perfume. He often thought she smelt very similar to the 'old lady'.

When Frank was in his teens, he used to call around for Katey after school on the off-chance she was ready to hang out. Sometimes her mother used to answer the door in her dressing gown, which didn't really bother Frank. In fact, he was sure all the kids that knocked on Katey's door, only did so to try and grab a glimpse of Denise, (Katey's mother), who always, without fail, wore next to nothing: a silky red full length nightgown with two protruding nipples begging to be grasped by finger and thumb. Even late afternoon; she was barely dressed. And her odour, well, it was so strong Frank often wondered how the rest of the family stood for it. He always used to say she had her own unique smell; a fragrance that cut through the air like a freak petrol-spillage at a garage forecourt.

Frank had his fingers crossed it would be a sunny-day that coming Saturday. He thought if it was to be a 'sunny one', it may be an opportunity for them to indulge in a walk and

talk, maybe even a late afternoon drink in
the Daff and Crown.

A perfect end to a perfect day, or could it
be taken a little further?

Chapter Five

Leaving mother's Friday

Frank dragged his old suitcase down the pathway towards his car, which was parked half up the curb to create more space on the road. He sighed, then levered his bag into the boot. "Well mother, I'll be off then,"

"You take-care son," she replied "and watch how you drive. You don't want to break anything before you get there."

"I won't mother. I'll be careful, don't worry."

Miss Langley stood at the foot of the pathway with one hand on her hip, fashioning a huge pair of denim-dungarees which almost disguised her nine-month old bump. Mary always wore a head scarf, too. Not because it was some sort of fashion, it was just better looking than sporting a forehead full of curlers for the whole street to witness, day in, day out.

"Bye Frank. Take care," She added

Mary wasn't too happy about her son moving away so soon after his release from prison. She thought it might be a little too sudden and that he may experience some sort of culture shock.

"Oh and Frank, give me a ring anytime if you need anything. Don't worry if it's late, I've a phone next to my bed."

"I will mother, I will; promise."

"Pedro will be back sometime today, so he will take good care of me should anything happen."

"Have you got a suitcase packed for hospital, just in case?"

"Yes Frank, I've done all that. Don't worry, I'm a big-girl now!"

"OK mother. Well, I'm off then. Say hello, or should I say hola, to Pedro for me." Frank smiled.

"Off you trot cheeky, and don't forget to give me a ring as soon as you get settled in ... and Frank."

"Yes mother!"

"Don't drink too much tonight. I know you said you're going to stop, but I know what it's like when you, Dave and Mark get together."

"... speak later mother!"

As Frank joined the petroleum fuelled archery's of urbanity, he observed the shape of his only available parent grow fainter and fainter, leaving only the shadow of a memory to keep him comfort for his short-trip to his new home.

There was a loud knock at the door and the whale of a Spanish accent:
"I'M HOME LOVE." It cried.
At the time, Mary was cooking her favourite snack: cheese on toast with brown-sauce on top.
"What the fuck?" Mary jumped out of her skin, nearly dropping her lunch all over the floor. "Bloody hell, my waters will definitely break today if I have any more shocks!"
She quickly opened the door for Pedro, but no sooner she did, her little Spanish friend jumped all over her and gave her the biggest hug she had ever received from a fellow human being.
"My love, how have you been? I love you my beautiful."
"Get in get in, we don't want the neighbours to come out again. They've already been twitching today."
"Twitching you say."
"Yes twitching ... never mind. I will tell you all about it later."

Mary gave Pedro a big hug, then dragged him into the front living room.

Approximately two weeks previous to Franks arrival, Pedro flew back home to help out with the family concern. The business in question was a small cocktail-bar on the west-coast of Spain, just ten minutes from Corunna. It was a nice place in all fairness, and Mary often wondered why he would want to leave such beautiful environment to settle down in an area like Smeggington. However, she never dug to deep in that department just in case she scared him off, after all, she was in her forties and wasn't likely, so she thought, to get another genuine partner if all failed with little-Pedro.

He was a hard worker was Pedro. He never drank alcohol or smoked cigarettes which made it easy for them save money for their unborn child. Mary loved him. He was a far cry from Frank's father who was a low life at best.

Frank senior left them suddenly back in 1983. It was a shock for Frank because he wasn't expecting it. As for Mary, well, read on and all will become clear.

It was a frosty morning that unforgettable day back in May, and Mrs. Langley wasn't in the mood for a game of verbal tennis with her son. Mary shouted up to Frank from the bottom of the stair case "Get up now! You must hurry, and I don't want any back-chat!"

Frank's wake-up call that morning was like a clap of thunder, bringing a very poignant moment in his sexy-dream, to a sudden end.

"Ok ok!" Frank screamed "*Chill the fuck out will ya*!" he whispered under his breath.

He wasn't what you call an 'early riser', was Frank, but on that occasion he had to make a valiant effort and drag himself down stairs.

As young Frank chomped away on his sausage and egg, he looked out the front window and thought to himself '*what a cold looking day it is*'. As he did, he suddenly noticed his Dad cycle down the entry, then out of the front gate. Frank thought nothing of it at the time, but when he got back from school later that day, he could sense something was up by the way his mother was sat on the arm of the sofa staring at the four walls.

Frank senior was a bastard. Not only did he try and make the front living room look like the inside of a public-house (burgundy flock wallpaper), he often raided their holiday savings

47

for the dreaded piss, too. So it was no surprise that Mary had kicked him out that morning.

Nobody actually quite knew what happened to Frank senior. He just disappeared off the face of the earth. However, there was rumor that he'd become homeless, which was a concern for Frank. Mary on the other hand couldn't give a monkeys'. He had been given numerous chances in the past, the last one being the proverbial straw and the camel's back.

Frank senior wasn't all bad I suppose. I mean, he did used to say grace before they ate together at the dinner table …which wasn't often. You see, Frank senior thought he was some sort of speech master. Why?
Because every time he delivered grace before their typical sausage and mash 'Sunday lunch extravaganza', it wouldn't be unusual for him to harp on about the day's events. This would always include an anecdote or two about one of his stupid pals, and how they always got into a fight every Saturday-night outside the chip-shop. Not exactly an extract from Corinthians, but unfortunately for the Langley's that was as good as it was ever going to get.

"My love my love, it's only been one week, but I have missed you so ... so much, yes?"

Mary sarcastically replied. "I've missed you too, Pedro. I've missed your big brown eyes and the fact you tell me you love me all the time."

"That's ok that's ok. You are my love and we will be three very soon, yes?"

"Yes, we will be three soon, but my waters might break at anytime Pedro so be prepared. You may be a father sooner than you think."

Pedro's face dropped.

"You must sit, you must sit. Mary, come ... sit in your favourite chair. I will get you some refreshments. I have brought some Spanish tea back so I will be treating you to a typical Spanish drink. Now sit, yes?"

Mary slowly sat down in her arm-chair and nodded in response to her fusspot Spanish boyfriend.

"Frank's back Pedro," she announced, "he came out of prison the other day, but it's ok. He has a small place down Edgewood so he won't be bothering us."

Obviously Frank and Pedro had never met, but Mary was worried that Frank may upset him and ruin it between them. Mary was very insecure that way. I mean, after the pain and grief she had to suffer with Frank-senior, who could blame her? Mary thought the best thing for Frank, when he got out of prison that was, would be for him to go straight to a rented room before they got under each other's feet.

"That's ok Mary. I will love to meet him. You can invite him over Sunday for dinner. I will cook a special Spanish treat. He will love, yes?"

"That sounds nice Pedro. I will let him know as soon as he's settled in ... *maybe you two will get on after all.*"

Pedro added "He will like the Spanish girls as well, yes? I will introduce him to Maria. He will like, yes?"

"Well let's just take it one step at a time. I think Frank needs to settle in first before he starts dating again."

"Of course, of course my love ... whatever you say." agreed Pedro.

Chapter Six

Number 13 Edgewood Avenue

Frank stood at the foot of number 13 and looked up at what was going to be his new home for the foreseeable future. He didn't have much in the way of furniture, just a few things to accommodate the emptiness of that lonely old room; a few basic necessities which he brought from his mother's house: bedding, a stereo unit and some cutlery.

He looked down at his new key fob which he obtained from the housing office that previous Monday afternoon. He then slowly made his way up the path towards the front door.

The front garden to the house was barely a garden: a six foot square patch of grass which just passed as a lawn, and a narrow winding footpath which ran adjacent to an overgrown hedge. Frank took deep-breath then let himself in the property. As his eye's adjusted to the light, he noticed the walls were covered with chipboard wallpaper and the floor was still lined with its original ceramic tile. The hallway was also shady and cold with a lingering smell of urine. Frank sensed this must have been from a consistent overuse of the downstairs toilet; something that would become the norm to him after a few days of residing at number 13.

Flat 1 was the first door on the right-hand side. It was the biggest room in the house with a huge bay window which overlooked the street. Frank felt quite lucky in one way, but unlucky in another. In one sense, he had the biggest room with lots of space to hold his little parties. On the other hand, he had the noise of passing traffic to contend with; that, and probably the undesirable sound effects from the loo.

Frank entered the room, put his bags on the floor and started to unpack his things. He put his stereo on the old side-board which somebody had kindly left behind for him and plugged it in. He switched the power on and pressed play. As he did, a familiar, but comforting track suddenly filled the air in the shape of 'The only Way is Up', by Yazz.

The weather which graced Edgewood Avenue that day was a typical autumn afternoon. The fresh aroma of decaying leaves occupied the atmosphere, and the light breeze tempted the dead leaves into a modus operandi: the magical Kathak of an Indian summer. Frank opened his window to invite mother-nature in: a fresh fragrance which moistened his lungs and tamed his heart. It was at that moment, he knew he was close to something special, something he couldn't quite put his finger on. He slouched backwards and fell onto his bed.

***

"My daddy can drink as much as he likes, and when he likes, and you can't stop him!"

"Your right there young Sarah; I can't stop him." Mark chuckled.

Sarah gave Mark the evils; a dead pan face which could send a shiver down the most hardened of spines.

"Don't talk about my Daddy like that you!"

Sarah then suddenly laughed out loud in Mark's face and ran into the kitchen, only this time, she was confronted by two of Dave's neighbours'.

"Ahhh the Pixy Pals, I saw them on TV this morning Sarah," announced Dot.

Chris and Dot propped up the sink unit, which was home to the remains of a greasy-spoon-special, and supped from Dave's private stash of cheap cider.

"And that Pixy on the front of your t-shirt," she added "is Mommy Pixy, is it not young Sarah?"

"Yes it is Mrs. Neighbour," she replied. "You're absolutely right.
And you, Mr. Neighbour, do you know who this is on the front of my t-shirt?"

"Well, I believe I'm sufficiently informed on such TV delights so I will hazard a guess ... Mrs. Pixy, young Sarah?" Chris turned around and smirked at Dot.

"How do you know my name, Mr. Neighbour?"

"Mrs. Neighbour told me some time ago, Sarah."

Chris chuckled to himself then took a small sip of cider.

"Well ok, but I'm only giving you permission to call me Sarah because Mrs. Neighbour has already told you my name ... and its Mommy Pixy to you, MR. NEIGHBOUR!"

Sarah stuck her tongue out at Chris then ran out into the back garden.

'Where's my burger, where's my burger,' She shouted "Dave, cook me a burger, now!"

Both Dot and Chris, with jugs of alcohol in hand, peered out of the kitchen window.

"Look at her Dot," whispered Chris "isn't she just adorable."

"Frank is a very lucky man. She's such a lovely child and wouldn't harm a fly," replied Dot.

***

Frank took a slow walk down the street, as he did, he glanced around at all the front gardens which seemed to roll-out from the foot of each door-way. They were very pretty and Frank could tell that the owners, or the tenants, took pride in how their houses and gardens looked. Frank peered over his shoulder at the front garden of number 13, it was a shit hole. He knew deep down he wasn't going to fix that dump up, not if the rest of the tenants couldn't be bothered.

Frank walked a little more towards the junction. As he did, he noticed a public phone box.

"Great," He said to himself. "I'll phone our mom and let her know that I'm all unpacked and settled in."

As Frank opened the door, he was suddenly overwhelmed by a unearthly oder. He looked down at his feet. To his horror, he realised he was stood in a puddle of liquid.

"For fucks sake, why do people do this?"

Frank tiptoed through the rancid urine and reached out for the hand piece, being extra careful not to disturb what could only be described as a mix of fresh vomit, and stale piss.

"Mom, mom, it's me … how are you?" The moment Frank heard his mother's voice on the other end of the line, he pushed a ten-pence-piece into the money slot.

"I'm not feeling great, Frank, but that's not going to last forever," Mary replied. How are you? Have you settled in yet?"

"Yes mother. I've unpacked all my things and arranged my room just the way I want it. It's not bad to be honest, you will have to come and see it sometime."

"Yes I will son. I just need to drop this baby and get back to some sort of norm, if that's in any way possible?"

"OH, and mother, I found the little present you hid in the bag. Thanks mom, I love it ... I'll wear it Saturday whilst I'm on my date with Katey."

Frank was on top of the world: he had a new girlfriend, all going well; a new tracksuit and a-party to look forward to that very night

.Yes, things were definitely looking up for Frank.

"A date already, Lucky you eh," Mary chuckled "listen, don't go overboard though will you. You've just got out of prison so don't dwell on the 'subject ' too much Frank ... if raise it at all."

Frank pulled the ear-piece away from his mouth then looked at it as if to say: 'yeah yeah, I get the drift'.

"And another thing, Frank, did I tell you we know the sex of the baby?"

"No, you didn't tell me that mother."

"Well it's a girl, Frank, and with your permission, we'd like to call her Sarah."

"That would be an honour mother, it really would. Thanks. Wow, a girl, I still can't believe it."

"Thank you, Frank, thank you. Oh, also, Pedro and I would like to invite you over for Sunday lunch this weekend. He's going to cook a special-Spanish meal, so it should be nice. What do you think?"

"Yeah man that's fresh, I mean cool," Frank replied. "Yeah, I'll definitely be there… wild horses couldn't stop me!"

Frank slammed down the receiver and jumped out onto the pavement, nearly stumbling into the road as he lost his footing on a wonky slab.

"Wow, that phone box fucking reeks to high heaven," he said to himself, as a passing dog walker gave him a dirty look. "Somebody should clean that shit hole up." The old man, disgusted with Frank's foul language, picked up the pace dragging his little pooch close behind.

"Shit!" Frank shouted out, "I've got to ring Dave!"

Realising this, he quickly made a second call, then buggered off home ... his visit, to what can only be described as the local public toilet, was finally over. His next chore on the list was to get his ass down the supermarket to do a little shopping, maybe stock up on some grog, a nick name for alcohol the three of them often used, and a few nibbles should they get the munches in the early hours of the morning. Either way, he was starting to settle back in to normal life, which for him, was a great relief.

When Frank was inside the nick, the prison therapist constantly reminded him that he may experience some mild-culture-shock on release. She said because he had spent so much time behind bars, the shock might be a little overwhelming at first. It could even have a delayed reaction and surface a day or so later. Frank never forgot the nugget of advice from Dr. Wesbold. Even when engrossed in an episode of 'Johnny Jill' at his mothers, he was aware that something may happen: an anxiety attack or maybe something along the lines of a flash-back; he dreaded to think.

Chapter Seven

Dave and his Neighbours

Dave sat on the back door step and munched away on his twelve-inch long hotdog. He also had his first lager of the night sat next to him on the slab, ready to be demolished. Saturated with brown sauce, which he thought was a mandatory gesture, especially when it came to the traditional 'fair-ground' style fodder, Chris tucked into his foot-long with a care free mouthful, chocking and spluttering as he forgot to swallow. He often said that the smell of burnt onions reminded him of the sea-side, and of course, the fair-ground, especially the one that used to take residence in the local park, once a year. The bonfire in question, however, was another story: a fifty-foot pile of logs which rested on a twenty-foot stack of wooden pallets; the ideal recipe for a ferocious fireball, no less. The vagabonds used to have a field day, as did the youth. Suddenly, cooking their own baked spuds in the remains of what can only be described as a 'public spectacle', became an interesting pass-time, even if the average age of the teenager involved was sixteen. The crates of lager also used to play a big part in them boozy-day's; crates of lager that nine times out of ten, was borrowed from the nearby off license, whether it was open for business, or not.

Dave's barbeques were the best on the manor. He rarely cooked extravagant food; there was just something in the air at the time that made them so special. The only thing that played on his mind, and left a nasty taste in his mouth, was the fact that Frank's daughter died after leaving one of them. It wasn't Dave's fault of course, and he didn't really blame himself, it was just, well, he couldn't help think of poor old Sarah and the fact her last day on earth, so to speak, happened to be in his back garden.

"You know something, Chris," Dave yawned, "I think I've had enough of eating for one night. I reckon it's time to hit the lager. What do you say?"

"I reckon you're right, Dave. Lucky enough I don't have to go out again tonight ... I managed to stock up the fridge ... ha!"

"Nice one, Chris! I'm hoping Frank as filled his fridge up too; enough for me and Mark to enjoy at least; don't fancy buying my own tonight ... ha ha."

"So you shouldn't mate, so you shouldn't. It's his party; he should supply the drink."

"I'll tell him you said that, and say hi for you as well, if you like?"

"Ha, tell him I'll buy him a few down the local if he's up for it. Just let us know when he's available, Dave."

"What's with all the hilarity?" Dot, still only dressed in a long t-shirt from her afternoon nap, showing off her aging, but slender legs, jumped off the step into the garden, like a leopard pouncing on its prey.

"Whoops a daisy, here she comes." Dave and Chris were propped up the fence like a pair of old washer woman on a gossip marathon.

"Fetch me a lager!" Dot shouted.

"get it your self ... Muppet!"

Dot slapped Chris around the back of the noggin. "stop showing off!"

She then slowly ran her heavily ringed fingers through Dave's hair, stroking his head like she would a lazy old cat.

"It's getting long, Davey, shouldn't you get it cut?"

"Maybe," Dave slowly backed away and reached for his can.

"Well, I really must make a move, Dot," He suddenly announced, changing the subject thus creating a little space between them.

"I've got to set the video before I go as well. I can't miss another episode of gladiators. I missed her last week."

"Missed who love."

"JET," Chris shouted from the kitchen door, "he likes Jet!"

"Oh yeah, and who's your favourite, Chris, Wolf?"

"Steady on woman, I'm a red blooded male is me."

"Get Dave a drink Chris … and behave."

"Dot, he's got to go out to see Frank. I don't want to be responsible for Dave missing the seven o'clock bus."

" … Ok, I'll let you off, but just this once!"

Yes, kind hearted and generous, they made Dave feel wanted and loved. It was just sometimes when Dot was a little pissed, he often wondered if she was trying to seduce him. He knew Chris was having trouble with the old pipes, so any thoughts leading down the path of maybe having a sprog of their own, was vastly becoming fantasy, unfortunately for Dot.

"See you later guys, I'm out of here."

Dave quickly jumped into the kitchen, bolted his door and pressed record on the video player.

"I must wash my hair when I get back home." He thought to himself.

Chapter Eight

Friday night: Party Night

"A little Happy Mondays I think to kick start the night."

Frank slowly slid a twelve-inch vinyl record out of its sleeve and placed it on his record deck.

"Yes, this should get me in the right mood for a party ... let the good times begin."

He turned the volume right up allowing 'Step On' to blast throughout the household and beyond.

The streets of Smeggington were like any other inner-city suburban streets; the people who dwelled there and the businesses that flourished, were very much connected. These were the very shops that you could buy an ice-cold beer to go with your morning paper ... a recipe for any 'budding alcoholic' to tinker with.

Most of the shop-owners were quite friendly. If you were a regular, you may have be lucky enough to get credit for booze. Of course, the closing times were always close to midnight so there was plenty of opportunity to become a fully-blown piss head.

However, Smeggington high street was a shadow of its former self. New businesses were appearing in the shape of the pound store; the back street second hand shop, which was once a prominent part of everyday life, back in the seventies and eighties, slowly disappeared making way for the bigger more modern version. Most of the big names were gone, and in their place was either the good old charity shop, or the all too familiar temporary businesses which maybe lasted a year or so. Some used to say it was a breeding ground for violence. And given ten years or so of local deprivation, the word one would use could only be described as 'inevitable'.

Bang; bang! There was a loud knock on the front door to number 13.

"What the bloody hell?"

Frank suddenly stopped what he was doing, which was desperately trying to learn the running man; a dance step which proved popular around the early nineties, and quickly turned his music down. But before rushing via the communal corridor to the front door, he took a cheeky peak through the curtains. As expected,

there, standing on his door-step, was Dave and
Mark. They were both rubbing their hands
together and breathing out condensation into the
night air. Frank suddenly banged the window
which caused Dave and Mark to quickly turn
their heads in a synchronized fashion.

"Oi oi!" Frank shouted.
"Oi oi!" They shouted back.
"Open up Frank, its bloody freezing out
here!" barked Dave.

Not taking his neighbours into
consideration for one minute, Frank quickly
darted towards the front door, grabbed the
handle and flung it open. Strangely enough,
when Frank found himself face-to-face with his
long lost pals, there was a moment's silence.

It was Mark who finally broke the
ice: "Well, aren't you going to invite us in
then?" He said.
"Come in, come in. Sorry, where's my
manners?"

The fact Frank had another shot at life, was
a great relief for Dave and Mark. They were,
however, worried about how he may be feeling

taking into account his absence from society. They were also curious as regards the subject of Sarah, and how he had come to terms, if at all, with the loss of his only daughter.

"So Frank, how does it feel, eh? How does it feel to be free, once again?

"It feels wonderful my friend. And what's more, I'm never going back inside, never!"

"We surely hope so mate, we surely do." replied Mark.

"That place was a right shithole," Growled Frank "I hated it, so much! But less about me for the moment; how have you guys been?"

"Well, you know me Frank," said Dave, "I've been busy working; paying my way in life. But it's a lot easier now I have a little helper on board."

Dave smirked at Frank, then turned towards Mark. "Isn't it Mark?"

Mark was grateful that Dave had gave him work, but he wasn't too happy about the way he treated him, and the way he spoke to him in front of people, especially Frank.

"...I gave my job up in book-binding, Frank," said Mark, "the old man didn't want me too, but I thought fuck it, you only live once."

"I bet he went ballistic mate. He used to love the fact you were a 'book-binder' ... for some reason."

"Yeah, for some reason," replied Mark "a reason I've never quite understood, to be honest."

"How you finding working with this slave driver anyway, is he treating you correctly?" Frank had a little snigger to himself, while Dave tried to change the subject at hand.

"Well, he's making money, that's the main thing. Anyway, Frank, aren't you drinking tonight? Mark and I had a can on the way here. I bumped into him on the bus, so we decided to spark-up a couple."

"I sure am drinking mate. Don't tell the old lady though; she'd lose her rag if she found out."

"Our lips are sealed." replied Dave.

It wasn't long before Dave and Mark found a place to park their back sides. Mark decided the floor might be the easy option for the time-being. The logic behind that was, if he did get a little tipsy, a little too soon, the deck would probably be the safest, and nearest place for him should he suddenly collapse. Dave on the other hand chose the end of the bed to park his rear. You see, there wasn't a chair to be seen in Frank's room, just a rickety old wooden bed. So it was a matter of first come, first serve, well, at least until Frank could get his act together in the way of purchasing a couple of beanbags. It was either that, or opt for 'Low Tech' (homemade furniture made from materials usually found in a well-stocked skip) to brighten up his room.

Frank decided to crank up the stereo. He thought he'd blast away some of their favourite tunes, which at that time of night was always going to be a decent chunk from Sabbath-Bloody-Sabbath. However, Mark had the foresight to bring his own music along. Oasis was the name of the band, and the title of the album was called Definitely Maybe.

"Frank, here ... put this on mate. Try track-three; you'll love it!"
"What's this mate? I thought I'd try a little Sabbath first to lift the mood."
"No, seriously, Frank," Dave butted in, "they're brilliant. It's just come out in the

shops. To be honest, I reckon they are going to be massive."

".... go on then." Frank slurred.

Frank took the tape from Mark and put it in the tape-deck, but before he pressed play, he turned to Mark and Dave to formally welcome them into his new home.

"So, gentlemen, here we are. It's a Friday night and we're finally together in my new humble abode. It's not much, I grant you, but given a little time I think I'll fall in love with this little place of mine. Welcome, my friends, to my new home." rhymed Frank.

"Ah, I feel prison has made you a little poetic, Frank."

"I'm not gay, David."

"I not suggesting that you are mate, I'm just saying."

Mark and Dave were the only friends he had contact with during his stay in prison. Mary on the other hand, Franks mother, didn't visit him once. Don't get me wrong, she obviously cared about her only son, but after Frank Senior had the pleasure of spending a few months in solitary for nearly beating her senseless one afternoon, she vowed never to step foot in one again. Shortly after that, she developed a strange phobia of anything prison-like. Frank didn't mind. He knew all about his mother's problem, so rarely brought the subject up.

"...You see, in the nick," Frank went on to say, "in the nick, I had a lot of free time on my hands, and the only thing I found that occupied my mind, and helped me forget, was reading. To be honest, the reading section in there wasn't actually 'Birmingham Central Library', if you know what I mean? So, I had to settle with the likes of Treasure Island and Cat in a God-dam Hat…. Jesus, I know them books, back-to-back!"

"Ha, ha, there you go again mate, rhyming away."

"Gentlemen," Frank sighed, "gentlemen, let's drink up and pray this year will bring health and prosperity, what's left of it, of course. A toast."

Dave and Mark smiled in agreement then raised their glasses.

"Cheers boys." The three of them clinked rims then knocked back the full contents in one foul swoop.

"And Frank," snapped Dave, "I hope this year will bring you the happiness you deserve, especially after what you've been through."

" ... and locked away in that stinking hole," added Mark "it must have been a nightmare, mate"

"Yes, Frank, we are both very sorry for what has happened. Poor old Sarah; may her soul rest in peace."

They sat in silence for a while and reflected on how things were very different, back in the day.

***

Frank and Dave finally entered the house via the front door checking the time on their way in. It was 12.20 pm so was time to light the barbeque.

Dave suggested that Mark put some music on; some Stone Roses to lift the mood a tad. That would buy him enough time to stoke up the coke in preparation for their burger and sausage experience. Waterfall, by The Stone Roses was to be the first choice that sunny afternoon, which was cool by Frank. Funny enough, it was the most played song on his car stereo which over a short period of time, rubbed off on his daughter, Sarah.

"How's it going, Mark?" said Frank.
"I'm a bit knackered actually from last night, but I should be ok after a few more of these, and a burger or two."

Mark waved a can of lager in front of Frank's face, and smiled.
"That should see me through until I get back home around tea time."
"If you get back home." added Frank.
"What do you mean 'if I get back home'?"
"Well every time Dave has a party or a barbeque, you always insist on staying behind after everybody else has gone home. Why is that, Mark?"

After the fun and rollicks of a successful BBQ, something quite bizarre used to happen with Dave and Mark. They would both disappear off the face of the earth for a short while where apparently nobody could find them. But as if by magic, usually about two hours later, he would suddenly appear out of nowhere, with Mark in-toe.

"I hope you're not suggesting that Dave and I are some sort of gay couple on the quiet, Frank?"

"I'm not suggesting anything of the sort, Mark. I'm just telling it the way it is. What's the matter, guilty conscience? Anyway, what's wrong with being gay?"

"Nothing at all mate … nothing at all. Look, if you must know I'm thinking of changing my career to landscape gardening and working with Dave. It's a far cry from 'bookbinding' but I can't do that all my life. That's why I've been spending most of my time with Dave over the past few weeks, Frank!"

"I don't know why you let your father dictate your career path for you," replied Frank, "you're old enough to make up your own mind or haven't you realised that yet!"

"Guys; guys; slow down, slow down, you've barely said hello to each other!" Dave intervened in his most diplomatic manner, treading carefully not to open a can of worms.

"Will you two get a hold of yourselves? Jesus, what's the problem now?"

***

The three of them stood up and raised their glasses in memory of Sarah.

"Thank you gentlemen, thank you. I don't know what I would've done without my friends over the last couple of years. You've been a real support to me while I've been in the nick. Nobody has wanted to know me, and who can blame them? A child killer! And my own daughter!"

Frank held the photo frame for a while, staring at the only thing that had mattered to him over the seven years previous to his spell in prison.

He took a deep breath, and forced a smile. "Let's not dwell on it too much tonight though eh gentlemen."

Frank put the photo back on the shelf then turned around to face his bewildered friends.

"Well, don't just stand there man. This lot's not going to drink itself!"

"CHEERS!" They each grabbed a can from the crate and cracked them open, simultaneously spitting froth everywhere in the process.

"Just one more thing, Frank,"

"What's that then, Mark?"

"Please don't ... and I think I'm speaking for both of us here, when I say, please don't disappear inside yourself, and fall prisoner to this room. Get out and about! Don't drink yourself to death! You've been given a fresh start, so take full advantage."

There was a moment's pause ...

"Again, my faithful friends, you're right. But tonight, we'll drink and get merry. We'll celebrate the future and what it holds for one-and-all. For me, a life time of abstinence. For my friends, well, I hope prosperity. Gentlemen let's get smashed one more time. Bottom's up boys, sorry, force of habit ..."

They all cheered and raised their glasses.

"A toast!" Dave announced. "Here's to a life time of abstinence for Frank."

"OK Mark," Snapped Frank, "let's get this music on of yours. I hope I like it."

Frank pressed play on the tape-deck. As he did, he read the titles on the back of the sleeve. The third track down was called 'Live Forever'; he turned to Mark as if to say: 'are you taking the piss!'

"Yeah, I like the sound of it mate, not too sure about the title though. You're not trying to be funny are you?"

Mark had a grin on his face which stretched from ear-to-ear, mildly resembling a young school boy who as just broke his virginity with the local slapper.

"Freedom mate, freedom. It fits your new-found freedom, 'live forever', don't you agree?" Mark quickly replied.

"Yeah … I know what you mean. Live forever as in, make a new life for myself and don't look back with anger."

"Exactly! Now, enough analysing and more music; Oasis are the new 'in' thing, Frank. Have you not heard of them?"

"No, I haven't to be honest mate. I've heard of that band called Blur though, they're supposed to be OK, and I think they're new as well."

Mark and David looked at each other and smiled.

"Forget about Blur mate, this is the band for you. You need to get into Oasis Frank. Remember that name; they're going to be massive."

"Ok mate, I'm all ears. Let's get it on."

'The sudden deafening tones of a heavy ride symbol and the unforgettable beat of a 18" floor tom gives birth to a new hard hitting vocal sound from the suburbs of Manchester. An original guitar riff and the melodic backing vocals offered up by a genius song writer that is Noel Gallagher, brings together the sleeping giant who call themselves oasis… live forever!'

"That sounds fresh, Mark. Yeah, I think I could like this."

"Yeah Frank, it's new in the shops now. It's got loads of good tracks on, but this is my favourite at the moment."

"Yeah I like it … it's a breath of fresh air. About time they brought some more decent rock music out. It's been a long time boys." replied Frank.

"Yeah, Led Zeppelin was the last big thing I was really into, although to be fair, there's been loads of good rock bands around; Sabbath, Priest to name but a few." stated Mark.

"The drum section of Pink-Floyd!"

"Great call Frank," snapped Dave, "let's keep this conversation geared towards Brummie artists!"

Frank, Dave and Mark all stood drinking their lager; reminiscing over rock bands from their childhood. The hours flew by and before they knew it, the midnight hour was upon them.

Turn of the night

The bedsit was looking frightfully messy by the time the main stash had been demolished. There were music-tapes all over the floor and the odd dirty magazine on the bed. For a good chunk of the night, Dave had been 'reading' from Frank's magazine collection. I think number 13 of 'Big, Bad and Easy' was the chosen issue, for some reason.

"Anyway guys!"

By now, Frank and his pals were a little worse for wear. They were half way through a bottle of Vodka, and ready to rumble.

"listen I forgot to tell you ... tell you," Frank went on to say, "I was up Smeggington the other day, and, and, I was surprised to see a new-vinyl shop open."

Dave replied, "Yeah, it's been there for age's mate."

He wasn't so drunk, Dave that is. Maybe it was because he'd paced his self, whereas Frank; he just guzzled the stuff down his throat like there was no tomorrow.

"Well, well, I wouldn't know, I've been in prison. Didn't I tell you?"

Mark looked at Dave, Dave looked at Mark. The only two in the room who were still compos mentis.

"But listen," he went on to say, "he had loads of chart music from the eighties man!"

"Oh here we go," said Mark, "I feel a Hip-Hop moment coming on."

"Now, you won't like this, Dave ... but I asked him if he had any Electro's in stock, and, and, you know what he said?"

Dave starred at Frank with a half-cocked grin, ready to bellow out an answer only a well-informed local to the area could ever muster up.

"He has the whole collection in his loft. They are worth loads. You won't get them anywhere. And they're rare as fuck. Something like that, Frank?"

"Yeah, exactly like that matey. How did you, did you know, Dave?"

"Because I went in there with my younger brother the other week, and after all the shit you fed him before you went away, regarding 'Street Sounds', well, it just stuck in his mind. I didn't know what he was talking about at the time, but now you mention it ..."

"Ha, well there you go then, I've convicted him!"

"Converted him I think you mean ... idiot!"

Dave turned around and gave Frank a dirty look. He couldn't stand the fact that his younger brother had been influenced by Frank in such a way, that it would persuade him to turn to the 'dark side', as Dave often gracefully put it. Hip-Hop was something that Dave hated. He was purely rock through-and-through. He just couldn't get his head around how people could be attracted to two, or three different types of genre at the same time ... he just couldn't understand it. Frank on the other hand, was quite open-minded. Don't get me wrong, he loved his rock-music and would never stray far from his deep rooted passion. But because Frank went through a Hip-Hop stage in the early eighties, it was inevitable he would reminisce from time-to-time indulging in the likes of Captain Rock, Grand Master Flash or a bit of 'Jam On It' from Nucleus.

'Hip Hop Be Bop … Don't Stop …'

Frank put a well know and therefore irritating classic on to irritate the boys.

"Oh no ... not this shit!" shouted Dave, "for fucks sake, Frank, couldn't you have choose something a little more toned down, so to speak. I reckon I could've stood 'The Message' by Grand Master, but this shit ... sounds like it's got dogs barking in the back ground."

"Ha ha dogs, that's effects mate. And let me tell you something ... listen to me. It was ground breaking at the time!"

Mark suddenly butted in. "So was Musical Youth, but you don't hear me playing their records over and over again, do you!"

"Shut up, Mark!" they both shouted.

Mark was a great rock fan, as was Dave and Frank, but this taboo was a group called Musical Youth. They were a Reggae outfit, but with a youthful twist. One of their number-one hits was a track called 'Pass the Dutchie', which was also Mark's favourite record. Every time he heard the song, he would do this little silly made up reggae dance which he thought was a great piece of work. He really thought he could dance like one of the 'reggae boys', he really did. Don't get me wrong, his heart was in it, but the motor skills which occupied the left side of his brain seemed to refuse him permission of ever becoming a natural mover.

"Ha ha, Marky Mark. I must confess, you do look silly when you do your little dance. I've got that tune on tape somewhere … I'll try and dig it out ..."

Oh no, not that as well," cried Dave. "I can't believe it. Let's get some Zeppelin on fast before we all go ga ga … for fucks sake!"

"Dam! I was hoping for a little reggae jam then. I could've done my little dance."

"Dave, get that Black Sabbath on quick before someone turns."

"Yeah man!"

04.00 am: The dead of the night

Frank woke up and managed to crawl into a squatting position, taking in all the magnificent sites of bed-sit squalor. Dave and Mark lay asleep on the floor like they'd been shot from close range by a blundering bank robber.

It was a frigging bomb site! The clock on the wall read 4.00 am, and the lamp in the corner was still burning bright; inviting three or four different species of moth to take up residence in his new home. He grinned, but then suddenly caught a glimpse of what looked like over-sized words slapped all over the walls in thick, dark red paint: 'SOON IT WILL BE YOUR TURN!' it read.

"What, in God's name …" Frank whispered under his stale alcoholic breath.

He rubbed his eyes then took a second look at the walls.

"Who's done this? You idiots, my landlords going to kill me if he finds the walls in this state already. And what exactly do you mean by that anyway: 'soon it will be your turn'?"

But there was no movement from his friends.

"What the fuck was you two thinking? He started shouting. "That's a horrible thing to say, man! Never mind painting it all over the walls in thick, red paint!"

Frank tried prodding his friends on the off chance they would stir, and finally light-up. But, unfortunately for Frank, they lay dead to the-world; dead with a trail of dribble from being too spaced-out to wipe away their own flem.

It was a shit hole! They were both surrounded by empty cans of lager and bottles of cider. And the more Frank tried to make sense of it all, the smell from the stale alcohol started to make him feel sick and disorientated. He cried out to Mark.

"Mark, for fucks sake man! I thought you were my friend!"

But the only reaction he got from him was a few of slurred words in the way of: "Father ... I'm sorry."

10.00AM THE NEXT MORNING

With one eye open, Frank turned his head and looked at the time. The clock read 10.00 am. He then let his head drop back onto the rug, thinking another five more minutes of sleep wouldn't go a miss. But as he did, he realized something wasn't quite sitting right in his room. He looked over at his pals. They were still flaked out on the floor, dead to the world. He quickly scrambled into an up-right position and cast a dark shadow over Dave, like an enormous tower block in the middle of a sun drenched council estate.

"You, the writing on the wall!" he shouted, "the writing on the wall! Tell me who done it, now! And don't dare tell me you have no idea what I'm talking about … because if you do!"

"What writing, Frank?"

Dave, still in a state of fantasy from one of his notorious sex and alcohol related dreams, suddenly shot up and confronted his pal about the unusual commotion.

"That writing, Dave!"
"What writing, Frank!"

Frank quickly turned and pointed towards the demonic graffiti, but there was nothing. The wall was pure white; a blank canvas and as clean as it was the day he clapped eyes on it.

"Yes Frank, what's your beef kido?"

Frank composed himself and took a deep breath. He then turned back around to face Dave, only this time, he started to get a little angry with him.

"One of you, or both of you, are playing a trick on me. You know what I've been going through the last couple of years; stuck in that hell-hole with nothing but an open-toilet in the room to keep me company. Do you know what they do to child killers in a place like that, even if is by accident ... well, do you?"

"Get up Mark we're going ... Frank's lost it."

Frank slowly started to get anxious and frustrated towards his 'friends'. He started to shout obscenities towards them, accusing them of painting the walls whilst he was asleep.

"You sick pair of twats ... how could you?"

Still half asleep himself, and now worried something was going to kick off, Mark tried to reason with Frank and calm things down.

"Frank, please listen. We haven't done anything, honestly."

Dave butted in, backing Mark's plee for peace.

"Come on, don't spoil it all now."
"Yeah Frank, we all had a skin full last night and none of us can remember a thing."
But Mark, in his infinite wisdom, took things a little far.
"Maybe you need to see a doctor, mate?"

"A doctor, a doctor! Get the hell out of here; you're both mad! And Mark,"

"Yes mate!"

"You're the one that needs the doctor hanging about with that nutter. Not me!"

Chapter Nine

Franks date with Katey

Frank stood in front of the wardrobe-door mirror, posing in his new shiny shell-suit. It was a nice surprise for Frank because he didn't really have much 'swag' to speak of, just a few scruffy old threads that kept him going before he was sentenced. Suffice to say, out of date and worst for wear.

Frank put his baseball cap on then turned it around so the peak faced backwards. It was the done-thing back in the early nineties, especially if you were a hip-hopster of some description. And if you could string a piece of Rappers Delight together whilst you strutted your stuff; you were automatically considered the dog's bollocks.

Frank squeezed into an old pair of old Nike Wimbledon. He looked cool; he looked cool and swathe with his modern day tracksuit; his cap on facing backwards and his retro trainers to boot. He was fit and ready for the day ahead of him, and what's more, he was dressed to impress. In a nut-shell, he was guaranteed to pull his long lost teenage crush, sexy Katey … or was he?

Frank stood at the foot of number 13, taking in all the natural, and unnatural sounds that were being fired in his direction: a car tooted its horn at another vehicle that drove past; the birds whistled their little hearts out which reminded him of times gone by: playing in the park with Sarah and pushing her on the baby-swings.

His mind started to wonder. He started to think about the barbeque and wished that Alison had kept Sarah back that day, and not let her go to Dave's in the first place. Maybe she should have known better? Frank was clutching at straws. He was looking for someone to point the finger at, but knew deep down he only had himself, and his drinking habits to blame.

"Well, may I say that is one of the most interesting barbeques I've ever seen, Dave."

"Thank you, Sarah. It means a lot when somebody gives me compliments on my work."

"That's ok, Dave. Now please, start it up ... I'm starving!"

"Ha ha, right you are, Sarah, anything you say."

Dave quickly poured the charcoal onto the empty grill, but left a little space to house a few broken firelighters. The barbeque didn't take much in the way of starting, however, the fire-lighter ratio to charcoal, was about seventy thirty, so as you can imagine, for the first five minutes it was ferocious yellow flame mimicking a very good rendition of St Vitus dance. In fact, it grew so big at one point, the flames started to lick the neighbour's brand-new close-boarding fence.

As Dot and Chris stepped outside into the back garden with their pint jugs full to the brim with cider, they took a gander around at the summer sky. Not a cloud in sight, just an evaporating jet stream which a 747 had kindly left behind for them.

"Watch our bloody fence, Dave!" screamed Chris.

"Don't worry," shouted Dave with a slight hint of panic in his voice, "it'll settle down soon. Don't worry!"

"*The guys barmy Chris, he really is.*" whispered Dot.

However, Dot and Chris were happy enough with their drink. And with the hot weather was so lush and tranquil, they couldn't even think of getting stressed out, especially with young Sarah in the near vicinity.

"What a gorgeous day it is today," said Dot, "best day of the year to-date I reckon."

"Certainly is, Dot. It's what life's all about relaxing on days like this. I wouldn't want to be working today that's for sure."

"To true Chris, to true - and you young Sarah, what have you got planned for later?"

"I'm going back to daddies to stay the night Dot," Sarah smiled then rubbed her tummy. "We're having curry," Sarah then held her index finger against her purse lips. *"But don't tell anybody, mommy doesn't like me having spicy food."*

"Your secret is safe with us young Sarah," promised Dot, as she turned to Chris with a cheeky smirk upon her face.

"Yes, I love curries," said Sarah.

"I'm so jealous," Dot added "I wish we could have a curry tonight, isn't that right, Chris."

"That's right, Dot, if only we could have a curry night as well."

Chris smiled then knocked back the rest of his cider. Sarah then laughed out loud in her famous high-pitch giggle, and bolted towards the house. As she did, Frank and Mark suddenly appeared from out of the kitchen looking rather cool amidst the midday shade.

"Ok lads, let's get this party started man," shouted Mark at the top of his voice.

"I one hundred percent agree with you there matey." added Chris.

"So guys," Frank announced, "here we are once again, sunning it up in Dave's back garden, and with plenty to drink. What more could one ask for?"

"I know what you mean, Frank; and as soon as I get this barbeque on the go we can help ourselves to some hard-core burgers."

"Ha, I love Dave when he says things like that. He's so silly Daddy."

"I know, Sarah, he certainly is different."

"Yeah, Dave; you are very different!" Mark smiled then slowly directed his head in Frank's direction.

"Don't even go there, Mark, you just ask for it sometimes!" snapped Frank.

"Ok peeps. Are you ready for the first sounds of the sizzler?"

Dave had a spatula in one hand, and a can of lager in the other. He was ready to toss the first of many burgers.

"Yeah bring it on!" they all shouted with glee.

Dave reached in to his tool-box and produced a small blunt wood-chisel. Frank chuckled.

"Bloody hell, Dave, couldn't you find anything less brash than that!"
"Well I find it does the trick, mate."

Dave placed the blunt edge of the chisel between two frozen burgers, then slapped the top-end with his other hand separating the two in the process.
Dave smiled.

"You see it works every time, Frank."

As Frank made his way down the street, he checked himself out in the reflection of the car windows; he was looking fresh. But as he walked on, he noticed a small sign tied onto the lamppost with an old boot lace. It read, 'Drinking and Driving Kills'. He took no notice and carried on walking, but the thoughts of young Sarah, lying dead in the road, slowly engulfed his mind. Frank started to get a little upset. He started to feel sorry for himself and slightly paranoid. He thought for a moment that everybody might be watching him from the comfort of their living rooms; peering out, making sure he wasn't getting up to mischief. This wasn't good for Frank, but he knew deep down he would have to put all that behind him and concentrate on what lay ahead, because if he didn't, any conversational gambits he might participate in with Katey that day, may quickly turn sour. He needed solace. Should he bear all to his teenage crush? Or should he keep his mouth shut and play it casual? Either way, Frank needed to get his act together and move his ass, because the time was now eleven thirty, and he had arranged to meet Katey at midday.

He finally located his car half way down Edgewood Avenue, sandwiched in between two four-by-fours leaving little room for him to reverse. But Frank being the great driver that he was, or so he thought, managed to negotiate his way out, enabling his little Escort to exhale, once again.

Frank drove off towards Smeggington hoping there might be a place for him to park near to the café. But the more he mulled over parking spaces and his rendezvous with Katey, the more he got himself into a tizz: he was still in a bad frame of mind and couldn't stop thinking about the previous night's escapades.

"I bet they had a right old giggle at my expense," Frank said to himself, "how could I have been so stupid? They were supposed to be my friends, for God's sake! Well, after all that nonsense, I have no friends anymore, apart from Katey that is. No, a true friend wouldn't do such a thing. A true friend wouldn't try and hurt somebody, and so deeply, just for a few giggles."

Frank suddenly found himself a little low in spirit. The words 'soon it will be your turn' started to roll around his head like a kiddies marble being dropped into an empty gold-fish bowl.

The High Street

After parking his car behind the supermarket, Frank swiftly made his way towards the cafe. But just before he went to cross the High-Street, he heard somebody shouting from in the direction of the old Church. Frank didn't have time for any nonsense, but was so mystified; he needed to know what was going on. So, at the danger of feeding his own curiosity, he stopped to find out what was occurring. As he did, he noticed a man, a scruffy looking excuse for a human being, standing on a small box. To Frank, it sounded like a drunken version of Question Time. He looked at his watch, he noticed he still had a couple of minutes spare so made his way over to have a sneaky listen.

"Hear this, hear this," the character cried. "What do the youngsters know today? That is the question. Is it just a second wave of what was and what shall forever be?"

Frank just stood there, bamboozled.

"Is it just old knowledge gift wrapped for modern times to see us through to the next wave of change and new ideas?"

He then went on to say.

"I often here the cries of frustration; change dished up on a hot plate of innocence, but I tell you this …"

Frank was so intrigued, but at the same time a little embarrassed at the fact he was the only one standing there giving the geezer the time of day.

"…the innocence that you quickly dismiss is our future, and the innocence that you carefully listen, is the red herring that I call ignorance!"

Frank shot off through the crowds of Saturday shoppers, narrowly missing tripping over a small push chair in the process. As he did, he noticed the cafe to his immediate right.

"Great." he said to himself.

He took a quick look around before entering the establishment, checking to see if Katey had been watching him, watching the tramp.

"Well hello there my gorgeous friend!" Frank shouted, which caused Katey to spit coffee all over the cafe floor.

"Oh you've made it then." She said, as she wiped her chest dry. "I was beginning to think you weren't coming ... that would have been a shame, Frankie boy."

Frank sat down and giggled to himself.

"Don't worry, Frank. I'm not going to bite your head off."

"Well Katey, how long have you been here?"

"Roughly this long, Frank."

Katey tipped her mug to reveal the last dribbles of coffee.

"I see, about ten minutes then. I'll go and get you a fresh one; same again, Katey?"

"Yeah same again, Frank, which is a coffee with one sugar."

"Right you are, Katey."

Whilst Frank stood at the counter waiting to be served, Katey took the opportunity to have a good look at him, and what he was wearing. She smiled then gazed out of the window; there wasn't one person dressed in a shell-suit that day. She turned back again, this time Frank was walking towards her holding two mugs, one of coffee and one of tea.

"There you go my lovely, get that inside you."

Katey was kitted out with a black pair of thigh-high leather boots, a tight pair of jeans and an oversized woolly jumper which gave just enough room to show off about 5 inches of blue denim. She still fashioned her eighties perm too.

So with that in mind, it almost gave the impression of an eighties throw-back, living in the early nineties.

"So Frank, tell me a little about yourself. What have you been getting up too over the past eight years?"

This was the moment Frank was dreading. Was he to go straight in with the truth, or was he to lie and risk everything.

"Did you ever marry, Frank?"

"Yes I did. I was married once, but we got divorced ... sadly."

"Any kids, Frank?"

And there was the bomb shell. He'd tripped himself up and there was no looking back. Frank had to tell the truth. He couldn't lie about such a thing, never.

"I have ... I did have a
child, yes." He muttered under his breath.

Katey lowered the mug away from her face then quickly slammed it back on the table.

"What!"

"I used to have a child, Katey, yes, but she got killed in a car crash two and a half years ago!" Frank forcefully added. "I don't like talking about it to be honest!"

"Oh my God, Frank, it must of terrible for you. I'm so sorry mate."

Katey then put her hands around Franks, both sharing an intimate moment before he pulled away to take another sup of his tea.

"But … that's in the past now. It's no use talking about it, not here and now anyway. Actually, I'd like to hear a little more about you, and what you've been up too."

Frank quickly steered the conversation in another direction. He didn't want the 'how did this happen, and were' scenario getting dragged up again. That being the case, he would have to tell the whole truth, regardless. But if he could get away with telling her that his daughter was dead, by bypassing all the other details, he may even still be in with a chance, even more so should he decide to play the sympathy card.

"It must have been terrible, Frank. To be honest, I'm having trouble coming to terms with it myself. You look so calm about it all though."

"Katey, it's been over two years now. Of course, I still have memories and even some flash-backs, but that's another story."

"I just can't ..."

"Please, Katey, let's change the subject. What's been happening with you over the last few years anyway ... married, kids?"

"Well, no. I was never married, Frank, and has for kids." Katey struggled with her words. "well ... I can't have them, Frank. I was tested a couple of months ago and the doctor reckons I'm sterile."

"Katey I'm sorry. I know it must be hard for a woman in them circumstances ... but you know."

"I know there's always adoption." Katey quickly replied.

Frank leaned back in his chair then slapped his hands on his thigh.

"Katey, just look at us, we're a-pair of hopeless cases aren't we. Let's start again eh!"

Frank started to laugh out loud. As he did, Katey joined him; cackling away at their premature 'awkward' moment.

"What are we like?" she said, "anyway, do you have a girlfriend?"

"No I haven't, and you?"

"No I haven't a girlfriend, Frank ... or a boy friend."

They both giggled.

"Katey, let's get out of here and go for a proper drink."

Frank grabbed Katey's hand a pulled her up from the table; momentarily displaying a flash of manliness; a moment he hoped might bring them closer physically: a touch of shoulder maybe, or even better, an accidental hug.

"But Frank, what about the coffee,"

"As I say, we'll get a proper drink in the pub down the road."

Katey giggled, but went with the flow. She knew at some point there was going be a little canoodling going on between them, be that a snog on the corner, or a fully blown sex-session back in Frank's bedsit.

As they both walked down the High-Street arm in arm, they reminisced about their school days and how they both missed them so much. Frank was trying to talk about his break-dancing escapades and how much people admired him for it, whereas Katey couldn't help recall the time Frank had a bad trip on magic-mushrooms.

It was about 1984 when Frank and his school pals decided to wag it for the day and visit the local park. They didn't miss out on anything important, just a planned trip to the local science-museum. Well, Frank and his pals had a trip planned of their own that day. They planned to a make a b-line down the only road they knew at the time: a visit to a magical-land only an 'LSD induced experience' could provide. This land wasn't a place you would like to visit often, however. This was a land where little green men would appear out of nowhere offering to take you back to their home planet. A place where giant pink elephants were often seen going about their daily business with one-or-two of their off-springs in toe. They would sing and dance to their favourite tune, Whiskey in the Jar, courtesy of a magical thumb-size Leprechaun and his golden olive-branch shaped flute.
Not quite the science-museum, but a lesson in life all the same; a lesson which would no doubt, alter the way they perceived our precious earth.

They must have picked about 200 that morning; and with the intelligence to bring used bread-bags to store them in, the plan rolled out smoothly.

They ended up going back to Frank's house whilst his mother was at work to make mushroom tea. It was Frank's idea at the time. He suggested they boil the mushrooms in a saucepan until the water turned a brownish colour, then pour the juice through a tea-towel as appose to a tea-strainer. As a result, they saved any unwanted bits to sit in their brew, and of course, got off their faces. It worked a treat. They all enjoyed the trip which lasted for about four hours. Frank's trip, on the other hand, lasted a little longer; six hours to be exact which left him completely stoned and paralyzed.

As they reached the end of the High-Street, Frank noticed it was starting to rain. He took off his tracksuit top and offered it to Katey, but to his surprise, Katey declined. She told him it was fine and it wouldn't be long until they reached The Daff and Crown. Frank was a little curious as to why Katey had turned down his very generous offer.

"I'm not being funny, Frank, but that shell suite isn't waterproof."

As Frank put his garment back on, he started to question Katey regarding her sudden dislike to his fresh swag.

"These are brand new, Katey, honest. Our mom brought-um for me."

"Frank, I'm not too sure if they're 'in' anymore. Take a look around you. Can you see anyone wearing shell-suits?"

Frank took a good look around at the passing public. There were young people on their day off from school hanging around the Precinct and looking rather cool, however, not one of them wearing a shell-suit. There were adults and pensioners alike, dressed in an array of different fashions; some modern and some from a by-gone era ... but no sign of a shell-suit. Just one dodgy looking character squatted on the floor next to the supermarket ... he wore a shell-suit. As they approached the pub, he managed to grab a glimpse of his reflection in a nearby shop window.

"Come on, Frank, don't get all paranoid on me now. You'll just have to live with it today. Maybe tomorrow you can have a sort out to see what you've got … maybe I can help you?"

"Maybe …" Moaned Frank.

The dull hustle and bustle going on outside in the High-Street was gracefully masked by the double doors of the pub. The fruit machine in the corner flashed its coloured lights repeating the same old tune, over and over again.

"I'll be back, I'll be back. I wish I had a penny for every time the machine said that!" snapped Katey.

"So Frankie ... Frank ... I heard you had a party last night?"

"How did you know that?"

"Well, I bumped into a said friend of yours on the way here. He was off to Marks to pick him up or something, but I managed to blag a lift off him. That's why I was in the cafe so early."

"So Dave brought you here. He didn't put you in the back did he like he often does with Mark."

"No, I was up front with him. I think he quite enjoyed it to be honest." Katey smugly revealed.

Franks face dropped. He didn't consider himself to be the jealous type, but he didn't like the idea of Dave trying to muscle in on his thing, especially after the previous night's escapades.

"What do you mean, he quite liked it. He didn't try anything on did he?"

"Don't be silly, Frank, why would he want to do that? And what could we have possibly got up to whilst he was driving? He did crack a silly comment though when I first got in the truck."

"…I wouldn't put anything past that twat," Frank butted in, "not after last night anyway. I thought he … well, I thought the both of them were my friends, but now I know better … what silly crack?"

"Well I'm not sure what he meant by it, but when I first sat down on the floor, he turned around and said to me: 'while you're down there love'. Katey smiled and took a sip of her drink.

"Eh, that's weird. Mind you, I've come to expect random comments from Dave and Mark over the last few years."

Frank took a deep breath then started to explain to Katey about how they were having a great time Friday night. He then went on to say how they wrote all over his walls whilst he was asleep. Not only that, the subject of the graffiti was so personal to him, he could never forgive them.

"But Frank, Dave told me you just woke up going mental. He said he thought you were having a nightmare or something until he quickly realized that you were being serious. That's why they left."

"The writing on the wall, Katey, it said: 'Soon, it will be your turn.' who would do such a thing to their friends? They're just playing tricks on me."

"Frank, nightmares can come across vivid you know. Even when you first wake up, they can still seem a little real … lucid even."

Frank dipped his head. Yet another embarrassing conversation which could potentially make him look like a fool.

"I'm one hundred percent positive I wasn't asleep, Katey. They wrote all over my walls whilst I was a sleep, then when I fell unconscious again, they wiped it off. It was a nasty trick to play. They did it Katey … they did it!"

"OK, Frank, whatever you say. Anyway, do you still fancy seeing that film today or what, I'm not sure I fancy it now. I think I would rather just get pissed. What about you?"

Frank smiled. He didn't really want to see the film anyway; he thought it would just waste valuable drinking/Katey time.

"I will go with whatever you want to go with sweet-heart, whatever you want."
"Thanks, Frank. You're so understanding."
"Oh, and Frank,"
"Yes, Katey."
"It was great bumping into you in the week. I couldn't have predicted it, seriously."
"I know, it was a great surprise for me too."

Frank raised his glass to Katey.

"To a strong friendship that will outlast any controversial interludes."
"Ditto! Now, watch my drink, I need to pop to the shop. I won't be long, Frank."
"What do you need, Katey, some fags? I'll buy you some from the machine if you like."
"No, I need some mints. I've a strange taste of salt in my mouth for some reason."

Before heading out onto the high street, Katey gently grasped the door-knob with her long sexy-fingers, and smiled. She then flung the door wide-open and stepped out into the rain. This sent a rush of adrenaline through Frank's body. He shivered, then looked up at the clock. It read1.00pm.

" … but why mints?" he whispered to himself, as he ambled towards the bar.

Chapter Ten

The Marky Mark

"This generation … rules the nation!"

A tall figure, all dressed up in his best swag, namely his one and only Adidas tracksuit slowly prepared to gracefully express his artistic side which he had created from a mixture of body-popping, and Ska. The Marky Mark, as he called it, was his signature dance to any Musical Youth song being blasted out.

"With version ..."

Mark paraded around his bedroom with his knee's bobbing up and down. He kept his arms stretched out in a crucifix type-stature, never moving them once as he navigated the furniture with military precision.

Step slide, he strutted in time to the tune, nearly tripping on the edge of carpet in all the excitement.

Bounce bounce, he travelled around again; and with the option of another four or five of his favourite songs on cue, he was no less in heaven than God was.

Bang bang, it was the sound of Mark's mother getting closer and closer. He stepped back and composed himself.

Bang bang, he felt his mother breathing down his neck. He quickly lowered the volume of the music giving Janis the obvious impression that he knew she was on his tale. He sat down and waited for the inevitable to happen.

"Mark!" she shouted.

"Yes mother." he quickly replied.

"Get your ass down stairs, Dave is at the door. Apparently you have work today."

Mark quickly sat up.

"Work," he said to himself, "but its Saturday ... oh yeah, I remember now. Jesus, how does he expect me to remember something like that after a night on the piss?"

"Come on, Mark, get down here, now!"

"Ok mother, stop shouting … for God's sake!"

Mark turned his music off and headed for the bedroom door.

"Surprise!" Suddenly, Dave burst in. "Oi oi; you're not doing anything you shouldn't are you?"

"And what exactly do you mean by that, Mr. Mellor?"

"Never mind mi-old mucka. Get your shoes on, or trainers; we have a fence to erect. Although, I have a sneaky feeling we are going to stop off at the pub sometime today!"

Unknown to Frank, Dave had become close friends with Katey whilst he was away in prison. In fact, he would probably go as far as to say they had something special going on.

When Dave dropped Katey off at the cafe earlier that day, he warned her that Frank hadn't had relations in over two years. He also told her that Frank was a little unhinged after the car crash, so should be extra careful not to lead him on in anyway.

"The pub, are we working or going to the pub?" Mark spat!

"You know what, Mark, I think we'll go to the pub. I can't miss out on Frank making a fool of himself, not after last night anyway!"

"Yeah, well, I'm not sure. He's liable to flip. All said though, he was a bit of an ass-hole last night. Let's do it! Fuck work. Let's trap to the Daff!"

Mark jumped up off the bed and into his usual state of readiness. "Let's go, Dave!" Mark grabbed his pork pie hat up off the speaker and slammed it on his head. "Can't go anywhere without mi pork-pie hat mate, you know what I'm like."

Dave lifted a brow then let out a deep sigh of contempt; the usual facial expression which was fitting if you were to spend more than two minutes in Marks presence. Poor old Mark, he was the innocent one really. Dave on the other hand often wondered why he ever let Mark work alongside of him. The truth have it, it was probably the fact that Dave could control and manipulate him to such an extent; he could almost treat him like a slave. This coupled with their casual friendship and the fact Mark wasn't the quickest out the traps, so to speak, found he was in control of most of the decision making, be it work orientated, or simply just on a social level.

Dave knew Mark was malleable as did his parents, that is, they knew Mark was a little vulnerable and should be careful to whom he mixed with. His parents also knew that their son was in bad company when with Dave. His father hated him, especially after he enticed him out of his safe career in book-binding, which he himself secured after a long hard chat with a female work-college.

"Got any cash, Mark?" announced Dave.

"I've got about ten pounds, probably just enough to buy a few rounds. Will that be enough? Or do you want me to borrow some more off our mom?"

"No, that should do fine. If I, if we need any more, we can always have a drive back to yours mate."

"Ok mate, sounds like a plan; a plan I'm starting to like, a lot!" Mark smiled then rubbed his hands together. "It looks like we are well and truly on the piss today, Dave."

"It sure does my little pork-pie hat-wearing amigo. Let's fuck off then. You can sit up front with me today in the pick-up. I think you deserve it. Besides ... it is raining outside."

"Cheers, Dave." replied Mark.

As Mark waited by the roadside for Dave to let him in his truck, he took a sneaky look back towards the house. It was at that moment he noticed his mother peering down at them from the upstairs window; watching them as they set

out on their mischievous journey
to Smeggington.

Mark's mother hated Dave, as did her
husband, Henry, but she never admitted it. She
just wanted Mark to be happy and if that meant a
friend who was to manipulate him on a regular
basis, and drink all his money, then so be
it. She was never really a fan of Mark settling
into the tedious life of book-binding, especially
when there was so much out there on offer. But
Mary being a little less street-wise than the
average married woman, wasn't quite sure how
to point Mark in the right direction. Not exactly
a stepping stone to a better walk of life, but
a stepping stone which would one
day confirm Mark was on the path to becoming
alcohol dependent.

*'I suppose that's the irony of a being fully
fledged drinker; one will never quite know
when one is an alcoholic, until it's too late. If we
did have the foresight to predict this (becoming
an alcoholic that is), we could inform our ten
year old children that they are already
alcoholics, but just don't know it yet. And, if
they did start drinking, it would kick start a part
of their brain which would give them a craving*

119

for alcohol, which in turn, would see them become avid drinkers for the rest of their natural lives. Alas, this life would bare them no real friendships, apart from the one that kept them company on a daily basis; a friend in the shape of a glass bottle' …

Chapter Eleven

Daff and Crown

"And that's how I became Smeggington's most
infamous break dancer."

Coming to the end of an interesting, but
tedious story about his own break dancing days,
Katey decided to stop him in mid-flight with a
curve ball of her own.

"Eh Frank, do you remember when I was
going out with Big Pete from the estate? Oh boy,
that was a long time ago, eh!"

Frank slowly rotated his glass, turned
his head and checked the time; an attempt to
distract her and guide her away from the
'painful' subject at hand, no less.

"Yeah, I remember him."

With a demeanour of sadness and his blood
temperature raised, Frank bowed his head down
towards the floor to try and hide his
embarrassment.
To cut a long story short, Frank dated a girl back
in the early eighties for about six months, but

had never made love to her in all that time. He really wanted to more than anything, but was too scared to try, just in case he couldn't get an erection. Suffice to say the said girl got a little bored of all the waiting around so turned to Big Pete, as he was commonly known, for certain gratification. Of course, Frank found out a couple of months later by one of his school friends that she went behind his back. He was devastated, but quickly got over it by striking up a new relationship with a sweet young girl going by the name Alison. The rest, as we say, is history.

Suddenly, Dave and Mark burst through the double doors, laughing and shouting causing the whole pub to sit up and take note. They made a quick dash towards the bar and ordered their usual tipple; two pints of lager and a packet of scratching. They scanned the area, desperately trying to locate the position of Katey and Frank, who, Unknown to them, were now walking on thin ice.

"OH for fucks sake!" Frank snapped, "Here we go. Now what do we do? I'm not drinking with these guys, not after last night."

After a short, but sweet hypnotic moment with Dave's ass, Katey quickly turned back to face Frank.

"Don't be silly, they're harmless. Let's just all get on and have a laugh eh."

Frank's stomach was now at the pits of desperation. His day had been ruined and what's more, he had a feeling that Katey fancied Dave. He even had a terrible feeling that Katey may have given Dave some pleasure whilst on their way to the cafe earlier that day.

Frank suddenly sat up from his seat.

"I'm going to the toilet, Katey!"

"There she is, Dave." Whispered Mark.

Mark and Dave moved in the direction of Katey; who by now was starting to get a little exited.

"May we?" said Dave.

"You may." replied Katey.

Two minutes later, Frank appeared from the direction of the toilets. He noticed the guys were sitting either side of Katey which made him feel pushed away and very jealous.

"Come and sit down, Frank. Don't be shy. They won't bite."

"Katey might though." giggled Dave.

Katey chuckled to herself then put her head on Dave's shoulders. Frank quickly grabbed a stool which occupied the adjacent table, and dragged it across. He reached for his drink which was near to Katey, then put it back down on a new beer matt which was closer to his new position on the table, and now probably the pecking order.

"What's the matter, Frank?" asked Dave, "didn't you sleep much last night?"

Franks face was a picture. "Now listen, last night was a bad experience for me. You did what you did for reasons I don't understand, but I'm willing to forgive you if you just drop it and stop harassing me."

"Frank, for the last time, we didn't paint words all over your wall! We were asleep like you. And how could we have possibly done it? We had no paint with us. You wasn't asleep for that long anyway!"

"We went through this last night. I didn't believe you then, and I don't believe you now. And what's more, what the fuck you doing here.

124

I'm on my date with Katey … isn't that right, Katey.

Frank quickly turned his head in the direction of his 'so called allie' for a nod of acceptance, but was suddenly faced with a vacant facial expression; a Mona Lisa special.

"So, you may as well go and sit elsewhere. In fact, go to another pub altogether."

"Cramping your style are we, Frank?" Dave then turned to Katey and produced his biggest, therefore most-cheesiest grin.

"We're not cramping your style are we, Katey?"

"No you're not, Davy, don't worry."

Mark suddenly butted in. "Ha ha ... and Dave give Katey a lift to the cafe this morning, Frank, did you know that?"

"Yes, I did know that, Mark, thank you very much."

Dave turned to Mark and gave him a serious look; a look you would only receive prior to a drunken brawl at the end of an all-day drinking session. But Mark was not affected by this. He just smiled at Dave then turned to Frank with an unusual look of his own; a somewhat independent smile which knew no boundaries. This usually meant only one thing. Whatever was to come out of his mouth in those next few moments, could either make, or break a situation.

"And Frank, did you know that Katey gave Dave a blow job this morning whilst he gave her lift to the cafe?"

Frank suddenly spat his drink all over the table.

"No, I didn't know that, Mark!"

Frank quickly swung his head in the direction of Katey, and screwed up his eyes.

"Oi you, Mark, shut the fuck up! He didn't do anything like that, Frank, believe me. He's shit stirring!"

"Mark, we're going!" ordered Dave, "just wait for me out side by the van. I'll see you in a minute!"

Mark necked the rest of his lager then slammed the glass on the table.

"And that's how you break the ice, my friends!"

Mark never really knew how to conduct himself in public, and in this instance, he surely didn't disappoint.

"See you outside, mate."
Mark walked towards the double doors.

"Wait for me around the corner by the pickup!" Shouted Dave, "I won't be long."

Dave leaned over and gave Katey a kiss on the lips; a soft tender kiss which lasted for about five seconds. This infuriated Frank, but he took a deep breath and kept his cool.

"I'm off to work now, Katey. I've got a little fencing job down by the estate. Apparently, a car smashed in to it last night knocking half of it down. Must have been a drunk driver!"

"I see you still have Mark wrapped around your little finger, Dave."

"It's none of your business, Frank. And what's more, he actually enjoys my company, unlike some people I know."

"What, he enjoys being bullied? That's a new one!" Frank laughed then winked at Katey.

"I'm not a bully mate, and I don't appreciate you throwing accusations around so loosely. It's not true, Katey, don't listen to him."

Katey lay back in her seat, crossed her legs then folded her arms.

"I'm not sure what's going on here to be honest. I just think you should all sit down and discuss the matter. After all, you're supposed to be friends, are you not?"

"We were friends Katey, we were," said Frank, "but after last night, we'll never speak again, and that's a fact!"

"See you later, Katey." mumbled Dave.

Frank and Katey were alone once again. They were left to pick up the pieces of a short, but effective conversation which had rendered them high and dry. Frank also had bad images of Katey giving Dave a blow job whilst bombing down Chestnut Road.

"Well thank God for that. I can't stand that twat. Mark's OK ... yeah, I like Mark, but that twat ... he can jump off a bridge for all I care."

"I thought you hated the both of them."

"I did, but Mark has given me a little reason to start liking him again. Yes, I think I could forgive him after today ... 'and that's how you break the ice' ha! He doesn't often speak, but when he does ... "

"I must admit, Frank. That was funny. It shut Dave right up."

"Katey, I don't want to sound like an old git, but did you …"

"No, I didn't! And let's change the subject before I lose my rag!"

"Ok ok, I'll speak of it no more."

"Good, now let's drink up and go for a walk. All this excitement has made me feel like I need fresh air ... and soon!"

"OK, Katey, let's go. Let's get out of here."

Frank grabbed Katey's hand and led her through the pub. But before they walked out into the world of high street depression, Frank turned around and asked Katey the 'big' question.

"Katey, are you sure you don't want my tracksuit top for cover, after all, it's still raining out there you know?"

They both stepped out on to the high street, only to be confronted by the noise of a hundred voices chattering; an amalgamation of idol banter with no limit of crap that was to be spoken. A fickle mind set which would command no more than a two minute subject in each blasé conversation. And at the risk of sounding intelligent, the price of bacon was brought up on the odd occasion to break the flow of endless words of lethargy. Only a loud bang could rescue them now from the sickly pollution. But with down town high street now pedestrianized, the chances of a car back firing seemed a far distant dream.

"Let's move our ass, Katey. I know a nice shop we can pop into. It'll keep us dry ... and sane, ha."

"Yeah, it does seem to be a little more noisy than usual around her today. Maybe it's my hangover?"

"I hear that!"

Just around the corner from the Daff was a little slip road where people could park their cars. It was only a small road; and with a public toilet perched at the end, it was very convenient for Daff drinkers should their shit hole be out of order. Dave's pickup truck was parked next to the toilet, half on, and half off the curb. Mark was sitting on an old bench which was situated next to it. He had his head in his hands and was tapping his foot on the floor.

As Dave made an appearance, Mark jumped up and stood to attention.

"There you are mate. What you doing sitting on the floor?"

"Well I thought..."

"You know what, Mark, you think too much sometimes. Let me give an example shall I. In the pub you opened your mouth about me having a blow job off Katey, didn't you!"

"Yeah, well..."

"And then what did you do, Mark? I'll tell you what 'you' did. You made me look like a fool in front of her, didn't you?"

"I didn't mean it, Dave, honest."

Dave looked down towards the floor for a second, contemplating whether to just walk away, or push the matter a little further.

"Mark, is it really how you break the ice?"

"It was a joke, mate."

"Well, I've got a joke for you right here on the end of my fist!"

With his scabby bare knuckles, which he obtained after smashing his own kitchen door in that previous week, he took a swing at Mark catching him right on the sweet-spot. This sent him flying to the deck faster than a game of fifty-two card pick-up.

It was a Monday evening when Dave and Mark decided to go for a few in the Daff. It was happy hour that night, which meant you could buy a pint of cider for about fifty pence; half the price to what it usually was any other time of the day. They both had a right good old laugh and a joke, and the more piss they got down them, the more they started to become foolish with their banter and third party ridiculing. But as the night wore on, Mark performed his usual trick by pretending to go to the toilet. He excused himself, as one does in them situations, but instead of heading towards the gents, he took a swift left and bolted out the emergency exit. Nobody could ever understand why Mark did this; and if he was ever quizzed about it the next day, he would just claim he had a black-out and couldn't remember what had happened. On that occasion though, it became apparent to Dave that Mark wasn't coming back from checking the plumbing, as he often put it. This enraged Dave. It enraged him to the point that when he got home, he flipped out smashing everything up in the kitchen. This ultimately left two huge 'fist-shaped' holes in the back-door for to see; cutting his knuckles up in the process.

As Dave made contact with Mark's face, he knocked him over, causing him to fall to the ground nearly hitting his head on the side of the public toilet. He cried out in pain. "No! Dave! Please ... leave me alone!" but as he did, the blood started to flow from his face, then on to his hands were he tried to protect himself from the wrath of his bully buddy. He tried to scuffle away from Dave in an attempt to save himself from another beating, but found it hard to move as Dave's fingers were clamped to his throat like a pair of mole-grips snapped into position.

"And that's how you break people's noses, mate!"

"I'm sorry, mate, I'm sorry. Please, don't hit me, please!" screamed Mark.

"Get your ass off the floor and into the back of the wagon. I'll take you home. Oh, and by the way, if you ever tell anyone about this, I'll come back at you tenfold. Do you understand?"

"Yeah, Dave, I understand. Sorry mate, it'll never happen again, I promise you."

"Good! Now get in the back. I'll drop you off at the bottom of your road, you can walk the rest of the way!"

Dave quickly jumped in the front and started up his motor. He put the car into reverse and slammed his foot down; wheel spinning out onto the main road nearly causing an accident with a crossing pedestrian.

"You see mate, you see, that would've been your fault if I would've ran the bloke over. Now keep your head down!"

Dave wasn't proud of what he did to Mark that day. On the other hand, he wasn't feeling remorseful either. It was if he was numb to the fact he was a control freak; a control freak that had just physically and probably mentally abused a close friend. Yes, I'm afraid Dave was just your typical bully who obviously had issues. To be honest, Mark never really stood a chance with Dave. One minute he was his best friend, the next, a person who you wouldn't wish on your worst enemy. This whole volatile relationship started in the early eighties and stretched right through into the early nineties; a relationship that would slowly become set in stone with no light at the end of the tunnel, unfortunately for Mark.

After the mornings unexpected Revelations in the Daff, Frank decided that a trip back to his bed sit wasn't such a 'good idea' after all. He wasn't sure how he felt about Katey now, especially after hearing that Dave's private bits may have been in her gob that very morning. In fact, he was quite disgusted, almost to the point of feeling nauseous, although, not quite sick enough to think about grabbing a little erotic fun of his own. In the back of his mind, he had a plan. An idea which would hopefully see the both of them locked in arms, deep in the murky depths of Lovers Alley.

There was a big furniture store towards the end of the High-Street that mainly sold beds. As a result of this, there always seem to be one or two disregarded mattresses dumped out back. It turned out to be an oasis for young gents and woman alike, who were desperate to break something other than a few school windows. Hence the name 'Lovers Alley'.

"Katey, Just a shot in the dark, but I wonder if 'Lovers Alley' is still there."

Frank smiled then turned away from Katey, hoping for an answer in the shape of a: 'yes it is!'

"Well, whatever do you mean, Frank?" Katey replied, "It's been a while since I've been down there. I suppose we could take a trip down 'memory lane' if you like?"

Frank humoured Katey. He had never been down 'Lover's Alley' with her, ever. So any comments like 'memory-lane' were just fictitious.

As they carried on walking and talking, Frank noticed in the corner of his eye two old knackered wooden gates. Frank nodded his head in the direction of the entrance, hoping Katey would get the gist and follow his train of thought. She looked up at Frank and smiled, then rolled her eyes. She then tugged on his t-shirt; the green-light to lead the way.

"Come on, Katey, quickly, don't give anybody a reason to become suspicious. Follow me ... hurry!"

They both jumped through the gate then closed it behind them.

"I feel like a little school girl, Frank."

"You'll feel like one soon enough, Katey … ha ha."

Frank dragged Katey off into one of the more narrow gullies which lead down towards an old run down shed. It was near to the back end of 'Second Choice', a charity shop which dedicated all its revenue to women who had suffered domestic abuse.

"In here," Frank said, "quickly, before the shop keepers see us and phone the police."

"Ok, I'm coming I'm coming. Bloody hell, I can't remember it being this dark and dirty."

"Oh ... it was always a little dirty as I remember it, Katey." replied Frank.

They were both stood in side a rundown old storage shed, which obviously belonged to the charity shop judging by the piles of old furniture: picture frames, boxes of ornaments, old stereo units and a wardrobe full of jackets.

"Bloody hell, I could do with a few of these things for my bedsit." said Frank.

"Frank, come here."

Katey made herself comfortable on an old wrought iron bed which was situated in the far corner away from the window. Frank took his tracksuit top off and placed it on the bed next to her, whilst Katey peeled off her extra-large jumper leaving her topless, apart from the black up-lift brazier she had strapped to her chest. He stood over her, grabbed her head then pushed it slowly towards his pelvic area.

"Oh, Frank." Katey whined.

Frank then suddenly pushed her on to the bed, creating an explosion of dust from the dirty old mattress. He dropped his trousers and climbed on top of her.

"Take them off," Frank whispered, "take them off."

Katey pealed her boots off, and threw them towards the doorway. She then, with the help of Frank's big, dirty shovel-like hands, wiggled out of her jeans faster than any challenge Houdini could have tackled. Fortunately for Frank, the tightness of her 501's meant her black lace knickers rolled down at the same time leaving her bottom half naked. Frank, with his right hand, massaged her soft dark pubic hair, touching, for one moment, her moistened clitoris.

"Oh that's nice, Frank." Katey purred like a spoilt moggy.

He started kissing her neck, then slowly made his way down towards her wobbly breasts. He rubbed them a little and made them act like two jellies sitting on a spin cycle. Suddenly, he grabbed hold of her bra strap and ripped it clean off, leaving her pert nipples on show, and fully erect. And like a puppy whose paw had just been trodden on by its owner, she yelped:

"Ouch!"

She was beautiful, and Frank had finally found himself in a position which he could've only have dreamt of over the years gone by.

"Not so rough, Frank!" She said.
"You always liked it a bit rough, Katey!"

Frank marvelled at his prize catch. She lay there like a good-un, waiting to have a good seeing to by her long lost pal.

"Well... what you waiting for?" Katey wasn't the most patient of people, but when it

came down to sex, she was all for a quick
thrashing: Wham, bam, thank you mam.

"This is what I've been waiting for!" Frank
shouted at the top of his voice.

He suddenly whipped out his penis and
waved it around in the air, creating a 'semi' for
her to grab hold of.

"Come on baby ... come over here and give
me a good seeing too."

Katey slowly started to widen her legs in an
attempt to entice him.

"Katey, wow, what can I say? You look so
... inviting just lying there on the bed with your
legs wide open. I feel so lucky. But Katey, what
has become of you?"

Frank took a cheeky peek out of the crack
in the door-way.

"... You know what, Katey, my old
friend. There was a time when I
would've jumped at the chance to bang the ass
off you. But now, well, it would feel like I'd be
letting myself down ... know what I mean?"
"Come on Frank, come here. Stop messing
about!"

Frank quickly gathered Katey's clothes together then chucked them out into the back yard. But unfortunately for her, they fell into a huge puddle of rain water; soaking them right through.

"Now what are you going to do. You lied to me and what's more, you had a blow job off Dave before our
date! That's fucking unforgivable!"

"What the fuck! You joking me about or what? Go and fetch them clothes back, now!"

"Ha ha, not a chance; get them yourself. And I wouldn't shout if I were you; they will hear!"

"Frank, please, go and get my cloths back ... please."

Katey suddenly jumped up off the bed and tried to run out side to retrieve her threads.

"You really thought I was going to have sex with you ... you slag!"

Frank stood in the door way and prevented Katey from being able to get out.

"I brought you here to teach you a lesson. To be fair, there was a point where I thought

141

'what the hell, just give her a good banging' but
..."

"You bastard!"

"...but after thinking of you and Dave, no chance! It just wouldn't be 'cool' Katey!"

"Oh Frank ... come on man!" she screamed.

"...and to think I used to love you. You're nothing but a slag, and a bad one at that!"

Frank took a full swing at Katey and knocked her to the floor. "Just look at you!"

Katey tried to stand back up, but kept slipping back over on a pile of old broom handles.

"I fucking hate you!" Katey cried, as she fumbled about trying to lever her naked body up off the floor.

"Watch them broom handles, Katey, you don't want to have an accident. Mind you, it might be the only fun you'll get around here today."

Not quite properly dressed himself, Frank quickly darted into the alleyway and made a b-line for the old tattered gates. He couldn't help but pat himself on the back as he started to pick up momentum. His cheesy smile protruded and grew wider and wider the faster he ran, just like Clark Kent metamorphosing into superman. Frank was so proud of himself, and by the time he had reached The High Street he was doubled up in pain from Cachinnation. He stopped to catch his breath for a second. He then looked back towards the battered old shed. There was no sign of Katey.

"Hopefully, that's the last I see of her!"

Chapter Twelve

On reflection

Frank sat down on his bed and reminisced over the day's events, desperately trying to make sense of what had happened with himself, and Katey.

Once again, he had failed in an attempt to go all the way with her. Or was it a failure? It was his own decision to knock her back, albeit an ugly affair. But the fact Dave had pleasured himself before Katey had even met Frank that day, was something he couldn't forgive her for. The only option Frank had, when it came to saving face, was to get his own back on Katey, which he did.

"It's just like a symphony," Frank said to himself "my life that is. It has all the ups and downs, twists and turns that Wolfgang Amadeus *Mozart* would be proud of."

Frank looked up at the picture of Sarah.

"And you my love; you were my inspiration."

Franks eye's started to glaze over.

"You were the heart of my arrangement. Everything I did, was because I loved you."

The tears slowly started to crawl down the side of Frank's face, then onto his pillow.

"We will be together one day my love ... I promise."

Frank shut his eyes and drifted back in time, two and a half years.

***

"This afternoon has been nice and relaxing, Dave. And I've topped up my tan as like you and Chris. I've also had my fair share of beer and burgers which is to your credit mate." said Frank.
"Cheers mate. But watch your driving going back. I don't want you getting nicked by the coppers."

"Don't be silly, Dave. I've only had two pints and even if I did get stopped, they wouldn't blame you. Anyway, don't worry I'm fine. It's you lot that needs to be supervised. God only knows what you're going to get up to when I'm gone?"

"What do you mean by that, Frank?" snapped Mark.

"Well the drinking doesn't stop in my absence, and it certainly doesn't get any calmer either, if you know what I mean?"

Chris and Dot suddenly laughed out loud at Mark and Frank's little exchange of words. They then drank the rest of their cider in a synchronized fashion, like two robots which had been programmed for one thing only ... getting pissed!

"We're going to love you and leave you now." chanted Chris and Dot, in their drunken attempt at singing their departure, instead of basically just saying goodbye.

"No problem neibouroonies. It's been a pleasure," replied Dave "it looks like you need a bit of an afternoon nap anyway to recharge your batteries."

"Your right there, Dave, we do need to get our heads down for a while. Maybe later if you're up for it we can have a few more drinks, that's if you and Mark are still standing, that is."

"HA HA I agree with you there, if they can still stand!"

"Ok Ok," Dave butted in, "so yeah, I might be up for it. Chris, just give us a shout later and I'll come out in the garden."

"Listen, I'll let you four plan your night. Unfortunately Sarah and I have to go. It sounds like the nights just beginning for some though; don't do anything I wouldn't do, will you Mark."

"Well, I might as well go home now then if that's the case."

"I'm not sure that's going to happen anytime in the near future." Frank replied.

Sarah suddenly popped up, "Daddy, I don't care about any of this rubbish, just get me out of here quick!"

With Sarah in his arms, Frank stood up and prepared for his anxiously awaited exit. He announced that it was now time for himself, and his daughter, to vacate the fun and frolics.

"Right, I'm off." announced Frank.

147

The five of them walked in toe through the communal pathway, welcoming the opportunity to briefly chill in the cool swirling breeze which often stalked the gate way to Dave's back garden. Then, it was out into the furnace which was the sunny side of Dave's house: the irrepressible front lawn untouched by playful antics, and still very much in its natural over-grown state.

"Now Frank ... I bet you wished you had air-con on a day like this, don't you!" Mark sarcastically commented.

"And give up the pleasure of driving a classic car."

Frank opened the rear door of his Mini and carefully put Sarah onto the back seat. He then climbed into the driver's side, and started the engine.

"See you later guys. It's been a great afternoon, and I reckon it's just what Sarah needed."

"No problem Frank," replied Dave, "anytime mate. Take care Son."

They all waved Frank and Sarah off on their short, but sweltering journey back home. Dave, Mark, Chris and Dot all stood side-by-side, smiling at Sarah as she waved back at them through the rear-window.

Chapter Thirteen

Event Horizon

"Wow, my first decent bit of luck all week."

Frank stepped out onto the pavement, took a deep breath then reached into his front pocket for his car key.

"At least I don't have to walk half a mile today," he said to himself, "Jesus, parking in this street is just a nightmare." But as he did, he suddenly realised he'd d left them on the mantelpiece inside the bedsit.

"For fucks sake, my memory is definitely on its way out."

He doubled back, being extra careful not to trip on the loose step, and made his way towards the front door. Luckily, the door was ajar so he was able to gain access without bothering Mr. Adams, a trusty neighbour who held the one and only master key. Frank quickly

entered his bedsit and grabbed his key, oblivious to what was splashed all over his walls, once again. This time, it read: "You are going to die, today!" Frank,
being unaware of the cruel, satanical graffiti, which decorated his messy little hovel like a sub way train in New York City, just waltzed on by without a care in the world.

Before he climbed into his car, he took one last look at the home he'd been allocated by Birmingham City Council: a terraced street which towered three stories high, if you were to count the attic that is. An all too familiar sight, which for some, was how the suburbs were meant to be; a cosy tight-knit community that didn't take too kindly to strangers. However, as he did, he suddenly noticed his curtains twitch.

"Eh, that's strange." he said to himself.

He quickly opened his car door, and sat inside, but couldn't help revert his gaze for a second time. There was nothing. The curtains were closed, just as he had left them.

"I must be going mad."

Suddenly, he heard a strange faint whispering sound floating on the breeze. He couldn't quite make out what it was. But the more he tried to blank it out, the more the ghostly echoes started to sound like the tortured susurration of a young child.

"Daddy ... Daddy ..." the voice whispered.

Frank squinted as his eyes adjusted to the sudden change in light. The street suddenly felt dark, like a dimmer switch that had been set to dusk to help cope with a thumping migraine. A huge black cloud suddenly formed and shrouded, what were only minutes ago, a soft blue back-drop. It was time for Frank to leave.

Half way down the street, he turned on his car radio.

"Oh great," he whispered to himself, "at last, some decent music. Maybe this will take my mind off the strange events that have been harassing me."

It was American Pie by Don McLean that was playing; a song which always seemed to relax Frank, for some reason.

As he rolled down the street, gradually getting comfortable with what lay ahead of him, he checked his rear mirror for hazards. But as he did, he suddenly found himself face-to-face with what looked like his dead daughter, who was sitting in the back seat, smiling. Frank's face dropped. He couldn't take his eyes off Sarah who was still wearing her pixy pals t-shirt, albeit torn to shreds and heavily blood stained. Frank turned around to take a look at the back seat, but there was nobody there. He turned to face the rear mirror once again, but this time he was confronted by a close up of his dead daughter's sick, pale complexion. She was smiling at him and laughing, laughing in her famous high-pitched giggle. Frank screamed out in a fit of panic: "oh my God! Please, no!" He took another look over his shoulder, but still nothing. He checked his rear mirror for a third time, but there she was, closer than ever; laughing and screaming at her silly daddy who was now in the starting position of having a nervous breakdown: "Daddy, daddy, look out!" Frank turned around to put his eyes back on the road, but it was too late. The brick wall which surrounded the local cemetery was about three-meters away from the front his car bonnet. The car collided off the road and hit the curb, catapulting Frank through the front windscreen, then onto the church gates impaling him on the rusty spikes. The wrought iron quickly turned from their original colour of hammerite black, to a rich burgundy from his pumping blood. His Escort carried on rolling, but hit the church wall, instantly smashing it to pieces and nearly causing a second incident with passing traffic. The car finally lay to rest on its roof next to an open grave; wheels spinning, and smoke bellowing.

Frank lifted his head for a last glimpse at the carnage he had created, albeit a sober effort: a smashed up Ford Escort, the blood from his very own veins running down from the entrance to the church, onto the pavement, then into the gutter to finally rest on a bed of dead pine-needles. Some passing folk going about their business stopped to try and help him, but it was all a little too late. Frank was dead! Only the feint sounds of Green Sleeves melodically drifting across town from a far distant ice cream van, hung in the air.

This brought home the reality of how innocence was once present in their-own lives, the hypnotic tones from the ice-cream van that is,and how lucky they were to have their 'own' children living a happy existence within a loving-family unit. And, without the threat of any outside influence that could smash their kindred spirit apart, like a priceless Victorian Vase slipping from a child's grasp, they were no less in heaven than God was.

CODA

Chapter Fourteen

Mary's House

It was dead on 2.00PM, which meant only one thing to Mary; time to make her special gravy in preparation for their unique Spanish cuisine.

Mary's gravy was a recipe which had been handed down to her from her mother. It was a recipe that, if made correctly, could blow any culinary wannabe to kingdom-cum leaving their gravy useful for only one thing ... the dogs bowl. Pedro wasn't expecting Mary to make her special concoction that day. He thought maybe she might give it a miss, after all, English gravy and Mediterranean deep-pan-fried fish, didn't really go together, did they?

It was all a desperate attempt to impress Frank to be honest. Mary was so worried about how Pedro was going to react - it almost knocked her sick that day. Pedro on the other hand was quite looking forward to it. He couldn't wait to get to know him, maybe even go for a couple of pints up the Daff and Crown, bonding like two typical Brits on a g-day (giro-day) all day session.

"Mary Mary, please, I will take care of everything. Just go and sit down, I will take care, yes?"

Pedro weaved his way into the kitchen, brushing up close to Mary's belly in the process.

"Watch my bump you!" cried Mary
"Don't worry don't worry," replied Pedro "please Mary, go and rest your feet. I will finish off in here, this is my treat. Go and rest please."
"Ok ok Pedro, keep your hair on."
"Keep my hair on you say?"
"Never mind my love. I'll go into the living-room and leave you in peace."
"Thank you my love, thank you."

The pair of them was desperately in love. It was just Mary, she couldn't really get used to being the one 'not' in control in her own kitchen. But this didn't matter too much. You see, she eventually got used to sharing-activities such as cooking and ironing with Pedro, all be them not quite up to her standards.

Pedro was brought up in a completely different environment to Frank-senior, luckily for Mary. They were worlds apart, which was a breath of fresh-air to her; a god-send if you like. This in turn created a unique experience for them, an experience which could only be described as an English/Spanish hybrid: Sunday lunch, fish and chips mixed with buckets of lager, fresh-fish, siesta and a smidgen of Spain's finest ... Calimocho.

Of course, a relationship wouldn't be complete without a good argument now and again. So, if monotony did ever get the better of them, it would always be left down to Mary to kick-start a row in Pedro's general direction. Again, luckily for Mary, Pedro wasn't the argumentative type. Unlike like Frank senior, he just used to step over the line and take things too far. This often left Mary in such a state, she would have to wait until a week or two had passed-by before she could leave the house. She often tried make-up, but it never really done the trick.

"Oh you are a darling Pedro. I can't wait. It's going to feel nice to sit around the table again, eating Sunday lunch; even if it is a Spanish effort." Mary whined.

Suddenly, there was a loud bang at the door.

"Ok ok, he is here!" panicked Mary.

"Sit down my love. I will go and let him in, just relax!"

As Pedro made his way through the hallway towards the front-door, he stopped to check himself in the mirror that was fitted into the coat-rack for such occasions. He was a little nervous too. Not surprising really, after all, this was the very moment he was finally going to meet Mary's son in the flesh.

Pedro slowly opened the door. As he did, he was suddenly confronted by an old scruffy character. He just stood there in front of him, swaying from side to side and drinking from brown paper bag. He was dressed in a long Khaki Piss-stained rain coat, which stank to high-heaven. He also fashioned an old pair of pin-striped trousers, which looked two sizes too big for him. His hair on the other hand was a completely different story. It was flat to the one side of his head indicating it hadn't been combed it in years. This nearly caused Pedro to burst out into a fit of laughter when he first opened the door, but being the gentleman he was, held back to create an air of dignity for the unwelcome guest.

"Hello, who are you?" Pedro said, almost chuckling to himself as he did.

"Sorry, have I the wrong house. I am looking for a woman named Mary Langley." slurred the stranger.

"Why yes, a Mary does live here. What is your business? I am her partner, I can help, yes?"

The stranger stared for a while then answered "My name is Frank. I used to be married to Mary ... a long time ago."

Pedro looked at him then smiled. "Is this some kind of 'English' joke?" he said.

"No sir." Frank replied, nearly falling over his own feet.

He then raised his left hand and pointed towards his ring finger.

"This is the only thing I have left to my name, which hasn't been sold for booze," Frank explained "I'm sorry for arriving unannounced, but I thought if I did call ahead, I wouldn't have been welcome."

Pedro started to become a little upset.

"I have a present for my son." he said, struggling to keep eye-contact with Pedro.

Frank senior then took an old photo of himself and his son, Frank JR, out of his pocket. It was an old picture of them both sitting on the back-door step to what must have been their new home at the time. Frank JR was holding his new toy-jeep which must have been brought for his 5th birthday. He was rolling it up and down his arm in a play-full motion, pretending it was part of some-sort of army maneuver. Frank senior on the other hand had his shirt-sleeves rolled up, looking down at his son and smiling; obviously he was a proud man that bright sunny day back in 1975.

"Those were the days," Frank senior muttered to himself, as he looked down at the photo "it's not much I grant you, but I think Frank might appreciate the thought, at least maybe for a few moments."

"Of course, yes ..."

Pedro started to get a little confused. He didn't know whether to just get rid of the character or call Mary to end the weirdness once and for all.

"Would you pass this on to Mary for me, if she isn't in?" said Frank senior.

"I will do more than that," Pedro said "I will go and get her, but be careful Frank, may I call you Frank?"

"Yes sir." replied Frank senior.

" ... Be careful not to upset her, she is nine months pregnant so could give birth at any time. I will pre-warn her though - soften the blow if you like."

"Thank you kind sir." said Frank Senior, as he bowed his head in gratitude.

As Pedro walked into the living room, he desperately tried to think of something appropriate to say to Mary, who by now, was full-on agitated by all the anticipation.

He slowly pushed the door open to the living room until he could see her.

"Well, where is he?" She said

"My love, I have a surprise for you." Pedro softly spoke "it is Frank my love, but ..."

But no soon as Mary heard the name Frank, she ran through the corridor towards the front door, but just before she opened it, she closed her eyes and took a deep breath.

"Ah, well, here we go. I do hope they'll get along."

Mary then opened it and produced a big, warm welcoming smile for her son Frank.

"Hello son, how are?"

Mary then opened her eyes and breathed out.

"What the fuck!" the look on her face, was one of shock "who the fuck are you?" she snapped.

"Hello Mary, it's been a long time. Sorry if I've caused any problems, but I wanted to give you this photo to give to Frank. It's an old photo, you may remember it."

"What, in God's name!" cried Mary, has she held onto her belly.

"I thought after seeing him throughout the week up Smeggington, he may like to have it, you know, for old time's sake."

Mary snatched the photo from Frank senior's hand.

"You've got a cheek haven't you, turning up at my front door like this, God, you stink of alcohol!"

"I'm sorry Mary, I really am, but I didn't know what else to do."

"Listen, I'll give this photo to Frank, but you ever walk down this path again, I won't be responsible for my actions. Is that clear?"

"Yes Mary, I promise. I will never walk down this path again."

Frank senior dipped his head then slowly plodded towards the front gate, but before he disappeared altogether, he turned around to

Mary for one last glimpse of what was once a promising future for himself, and his family.

"I'm sorry love." He smiled, then slowly walked away, head down and hands in pocket.

"Frank!"

"Yes Mary."

"Thanks, he will like this very much. I'll put it on the side-board so he can see it as he walks in, but Frank, don't ever do this again, do you hear!"

Frank nodded his head then walked off in the direction of Smeggington, never to be seen again, just like he'd promised.

It was an upsetting moment for her, not just because Pedro was there; it also brought back memories of a once forgotten family nest. But Frank senior had achieved what he had set out to do and that was to make sure he passed on the photo to Mary so his son could hang onto it as a keep-sake. And Pedro, well, he was still in shock. He wasn't used to living his life like a TV soap-opera, but this was something he would have to get used too, especially if he wanted his relationship with Mary to stay on track.

"Pedro, I'm sorry." said Mary, as she plodded back into the living-room.

"That's ok my love, I think I'm used to all the English drama now, although, it was a bit of a shock ... yes."

"You know what Pedro, it was a shock, but something else is bothering me now."

"What's that my love?"

"Well, we won't be able to have dinner today after all." Mary calmly but firmly stated.

"Why my love, Frank will be her in a minute."

"Yes, but my waters have just broken in all the shock, so Frank will have to wait now.

"Oh my God! Mary, sit-down and I'll call an ambulance. No wait we have a car don't we?"

"Calm down Pedro, you know what to do. We've rehearsed it enough times."

Pedro rushed up stairs and grabbed her suit-case and a couple of other things he thought she may need. He then ran back down stairs, nearly tangling himself with the bag handles in the process, and grabbed the car keys off the bureau.

"Don't worry Pedro" said Mary, as she franticly searched for her writing pad and pen "I'll write a note and leave it on the door for Frank, and Pedro,"

"Yes love."

"I love you babe, but please get a move on, I'm in fucking in agony here!"

The pair of them left sharpish, leaving the curtain twitchers to have a good old nose at poor old Mary as she fumbled to get into the back-seat of Pedro's little old Fiat.

"Maybe we should have phoned an ambulance after all!" Mary whispered to herself.

R.I.P. Frank JR, Long live Sarah Langley the 2nd.

The End

Printed in Great Britain
by Amazon

56594802R00095